Melville Best Anderson, Paul de Rémusat

Thiers

Melville Best Anderson, Paul de Rémusat

Thiers

ISBN/EAN: 9783337366421

Printed in Europe, USA, Canada, Australia, Japan

Cover: Foto ©Andreas Hilbeck / pixelio.de

More available books at **www.hansebooks.com**

The Great French Writers

THIERS

BY

PAUL DE REMUSAT

SENATOR

TRANSLATED BY

MELVILLE B. ANDERSON

TRANSLATOR OF HUGO'S "SHAKESPEARE"

CHICAGO

A. C. McCLURG AND COMPANY

1889

CONTENTS.

                                                                              PAGE

TRANSLATOR'S NOTE 7

INTRODUCTION 9

CHAPTER

    I. THE RESTORATION 13

   II. THE JULY GOVERNMENT 47

  III. THE REPUBLIC OF 1848 99

  IV. THE EMPIRE (1851–1863) 124

   V. THE EMPIRE (1863–1870) 142

  VI. THE WAR 177

 VII. THE THIRD REPUBLIC 200

VIII. RETIREMENT AND DEATH 223

INDEX 235

TRANSLATOR'S NOTE.

As this volume is the longest of the series, the American publishers have urged the translator to study precision, and to omit redundancies, repetitions, and slight particulars likely to be of little interest to American readers. Any one who takes pains to compare this version with the original will therefore discover that phrases and sentences are here and there omitted or greatly abbreviated. These excisions have, however, not been wantonly made; on the contrary, the translator is able to give a good reason for every one of them, and believes the book to be rather improved than impaired by them.

THIERS.

INTRODUCTION.

IF the art of writing consisted merely in clothing an ingenious thought in correct and elegant phrases, or in running down a new image, a happily chosen metaphor, there would be few great writers, and it would be something of a paradox to place M. Thiers in their select company. Critics would point out that the literary style of this statesman is not always perfectly correct, — that it sometimes lacks elegance or rapidity or picturesqueness. Facts and things, rather than words, stir his imagination, which is not reflected in his style. Strewn negligently here and there are lumbering sentences, colorless expressions, commonplaces of diction and thought.

Luckily, however, the qualities of the great writer are of an order very much above anything that can be taught in books of rhetoric. The processes of the art of writing are as various as the minds of which that art is the most splendid manifestation; and if some of the qualities that make the Racines and the Boileaus are lacking to the historian of the Revolution and of the Empire, as they were lacking to Saint-Simon, the merits which characterize him are none the less precious. Without obvious search after effect, without apparent art, he develops with breadth and clearness a vast narrative which he really controls as a master, while it seems to hurry him away as it hurries away his reader. The profusion of detail does not slacken the general movement, and this majestic river — this noble Loire which rolls so broad a stream — sweeps along like a torrent. Under a somewhat cold coloring, the concealed passion of the author for his subject animates the entire work. And what a work! Ten volumes on the history of the Revolution, and twenty on the Consulate and the Empire! This last work is especially pervaded with that hidden warmth, and may be considered as the most magnificent monument of contemporary literature. Deservedly has the French Academy crowned this work with its sanction. Perhaps no writer's vigor was ever so sustained throughout a quarter of a century; indeed, his last books surpass the first in energy, interest, and inspiration. Is not all this a compen-

sation for some redundancies, for some trite
moral reflections, for some deficiency in that
rhetorical element of which Tacitus has too
much?

And the speeches! Because an opinion has
been pronounced in public instead of being
written or dictated in solitude, is it any the less
a literary work? Since M. Thiers' speeches,
in cold type, are models of clearness and of
excellent arrangement; since in reading them
we are still fascinated as when we heard them
issue, in Southern accent, from those thin, expressive lips; since the fifteen volumes published under the competent editorship of M.
Calmon[1] form a course of judicious politics,
of well-balanced finance, of free and wise
government; and since this course is useful to
succeeding generations, — is it the less just to
point out their merits and to write their history, even their literary history?

The life of the man of letters is intimately
associated with the genesis of his works, and
one of the superiorities of the modern critical
method consists in not separating the man
from his works. First Voltaire, afterward
Villemain and Sainte-Beuve, gave us model-
of this kind of criticism. Here its neces
ـ ـ
ois de

[1] Discours parlementaires de M. Thiers, publiés, Paris,
Calmon. 15 vols. 8ᵛᵒ. Paris, C. Lévy, 1879–188? 1874.

is still more evident, for all the writings of
M. Thiers are at the same time actions; he
not only related history, he made it. We
must, however, limit ourselves and resist the
pleasure, somewhat mingled with pain, of relating the whole history of France for sixty
years. Although we are dealing with an orator, it is no oratorical device to say that in
these pages details will be given only in so far
as they directly concern his person or his just
claim to renown. Space is wanting to go beyond this and to break down the very thin
partition which divides the history of such
a man from the history of his country.

CHAPTER I.

IT was in 1823 that the name "Thiers" first caught the public eye; at least, it was then for the first time printed on the cover of a book. The title was "The Pyrenees,"[1] and although several passages have been adopted into the guide-books as the best descriptions of the vale of Argelès and of the plain of Tarbes, the work was not written for tourists. This narrative of a journey made in the autumn of 1822 is essentially a political pamphlet against the Spanish War, — a war not yet begun, but for which the active preparations were the signal for a great outburst of Absolutist passions and claims. It was not until the month of March, 1823, that the Duke of Angoulême set out; but there had already been a great discussion in the Chambers, and a ministry had fallen. The time was therefore

---

[1] Les Pyrénées et le midi de la France pendant les mois de novembre et de décembre, 1822. Par A. Thiers, 8ᵛᵒ, Paris, chez Ponthieu, 1823. This work was reprinted in 1874.

favorable for a summary of the impressions
which the sight of the menaced regions might
make upon an enlightened mind. The French
court and the Chambers had determined to
re-enthrone King Ferdinand VII., who had
been dismissed by his subjects. This was a
strange undertaking at a time when constitutional principles were beginning to prevail
again, — especially strange on the part of a
people which had more than once recognized
that a nation belongs to itself alone. It is true
that the Emigrants were loath to admit this
right, and that the House of Bourbon, reinstated by foreign power, saw in it an indirect
condemnation of their hopes and of their proceedings for thirty years back. The Restoration was itself a great example of intervention,
but its first care should have been to make
men forget this. Such a care would have
been in harmony with justice, morality, reason,
and good policy, — things which, whatever
people may say, are very often found in agreement. It was necessary, under the Charter, to
recognize in nations the right of enjoying political liberty, and of using force in certain cases
in the service of this right. Had the question
been merely to support a threatened king upon
his throne, the policy might have been more
defensible. But a French army was being sent

into Spain to give back to a dethroned king the absolute sovereignty of which he had been deprived by his subjects. Every liberal-minded man shuddered at this; and stirring debates took place in the two Chambers.

The occasion was excellent for entering the field of political controversy. But M. Thiers attacked the projected war not as a political theorist; much rather he ridiculed the "soldiers of the faith" with graceful wit and easy banter. This good-nature is a great quality in a politician; M. Thiers retained it throughout all the storms of his life, and to the very last owed to it parliamentary and popular successes. Fifty years later he was to say on a certain solemn occasion, "We should take everything seriously, nothing tragically." Such cheerfulness is one of the forms of courage, and is perhaps, together with intelligence, the most marked trait of his first book. A little searching discloses other qualities that are also to reappear later, — a style which, if a trifle lumbering, is easy and natural, and which seems the proper language of good sense; an interest in everything, — art, science, the industries, whose processes he describes in detail. There is a page, for example, on the manufacture of soda at Marseilles, that seems a kind of prophecy of those copious explanations concerning tissues, metals, and raw materials, which have given so much instruction to our contemporaries. One would be tempted to copy entire pages but for the fact that in the course of this study the opportunity will frequently present itself of citing the opinions of M. Thiers in his own words, of transcribing speeches characterized by a happy union of practice and theory, pervaded with the noblest sentiments, and strewn with brilliant, almost poetical, descriptions. It was not in vain that he was a child of the South; in his veins flowed some drops of the blood of André Chénier.

This was not the first writing of the young graduate of the Marseilles Lyceum. Louis Adolphe Thiers was born at Marseilles, April 15, 1797, and after a brilliant career at college went to Aix, where he pursued the study of the law. Scarcely had he, in 1820, attained the degree of licentiate, when he competed for a prize offered by the Academy of Aix. His discourse, a eulogy of Vauvenargues, was pronounced the best. But provincial academies were then sometimes tainted by the coterie spirit, and the Academy of Aix retained some affection for the Old Régime. M. Thiers could not have lived, young, active, impetuous, in the circles, and perhaps too in the *cafés*, of a little city that plumed itself upon being a centre of letters and wit, without becoming known and liked, nor without giving some promise of talent. He was looked upon as one of the Liberal leaders in a society which was still stirred by the passions of 1815. A member of the Academy, M. d'Arlatan de Lauris, an enlightened magistrate, having through excess of kindness betrayed the incognito, the Academy refused, for want of sufficiently distinguished contestants, to confer the prize; and the competition was postponed until the following year. A year later M. Thiers sent back the first discourse without concealing his name, and composed a second, which was sent indirectly from Paris and was without signature. The triumphant Academy awarded the prize to the second, while it put off the former and better of the two with an *accessit*. "The Constitutionnel" afterward gave an extract from it, which we perhaps do wrong not to transcribe. But these youthful works of eminent men are a little deceptive, so wholly do we find their authors in them. One would prefer to believe that study, experience, life, create qualities, or at least so develop as to transform them. The course of existence, however, appears merely to bring confidence, opportunities for the display of talent, sureness of expression; and it is not certain that M. Thiers has at any time spoken of the moralists with greater simplicity or grace.

Without dwelling upon this formative period, we should from this moment place beside M. Thiers his contemporary, M. Mignet. To the last day he loved with unalterable affection this devoted companion, — and this is rather a trait of his character than an incident of his biography. That mobile, active spirit which is to be agitated by so many great events, "whence so many passions and works shall bud and blossom," this man who is to know throughout half a century fortune and disgrace, exile and power, public favor and pitiless unpopularity, will remain faithful to the noble friendships formed in childhood and youth. These he kept, as he kept unimpaired the most serious of the opinions which he embraced with equal warmth. In his life separations and ruptures were rare. He was certainly not incapable of severity toward men; but one must have very deeply offended him in order to incur his ill-will. Not merely for his friends, — to whom he pardoned everything, permitted everything, — but for those whom he had once taken into favor, for those who exhibited attachment toward him for a single day, he had an inexhaustible fund of indulgence. If he avenged himself for a betrayal or for unhandsome usage, it was only by some innocent epigram. A hundred examples might be cited; here is one of the slightest: M. Berger (*anglicé* Shepherd), an opposition deputy under the July monarchy, was one of his faithful ones. Throughout many years, Thiers had shown and proved his friendship for Berger. After the *coup d'état*, when Thiers was in exile, Berger chose his time to go over publicly to the Empire. Not long thereafter the former deputy, without precisely returning to his old-time liberalism, asked a common friend to find out how his former patron felt, and whether it was still possible to be received into favor. "Tell him that I still call him my faithful shepherd," replied M. Thiers; and all was forgotten.

In M. Mignet, Thiers never had anything to forget or to pardon; antiquity has left us no nobler example of friendship. The contrast was great between these two men, both in physical appearance and in their mental make-up. But besides that natural sympathy which the ablest psychologists can only affirm, not explain, they had those common aims and aversions which constitute, according to Cicero, the first condition of friendship, — *eadem velle*, *eadem nolle*. Between these two so different

beings the conformity of sentiment was and remained so absolute that as they entered upon
life each wrote a history of the French Revolution conceived in the spirit of the other;
and the octogenarian survivor was able to
correct with his own hand and to publish
the last political writing of his friend, without
provoking any criticism or arousing any suspicion of a single alteration in the thought or
intentions of the author. Pylades never did
as much for Orestes.

In 1820 or 1821, M. Thiers and M. Mignet,
already inseparable, discovered simultaneously
that they were not suited to the Bar, and decided to go up to Paris. They had, however,
pleaded once, and in the same case; at least
Thiers told the story without being disputed
by his friend. They were to defend a man
accused of arson and of murder, both crimes
punishable with death. On the first head, after
a plea by Thiers, the man was acquitted; on
the second, in spite of a defence presented by
M. Mignet, he was condemned. He was pardoned however, because, said Thiers, it was
proved that the judges were mistaken. Disturbed by the pleadings, they had believed
him innocent where he was guilty, guilty where
he was innocent. Seduction had triumphed
over cold logic.

The account of the journey to the Pyrenees was merely a collection of articles first published in the "Constitutionnel," — a journal whose columns were opened to Thiers through the good offices of M. Manuel, his fellow-countryman. At the same time he wrote the political bulletins for the "Tablettes Universelles," — a weekly review founded by M. Coste. His articles in the "Constitutionnel" were spirited but serious; those in the "Tablettes" were in an entirely different tone. Were the glory for him less slight, it might be mentioned that he invented that lighter journalism which has flourished so much latterly. He gave those details, at that time novel, of which the daily life of governments is made up, — all the little particulars of the secret part of public affairs, of the interior movements of the ministerial council and of the diplomatic conferences. These articles received added zest when it became known that the writer drew his information from the copious source which M. de Talleyrand, in his irritation, had opened; for Talleyrand had liked Thiers from the first. The latter even went so far as to print an ironical article on the account of a journey to Brussels and Ghent which King Louis XVIII. had just published, and so wounded the vanity of the author, more sensitive than that of the king. What was more delicate still, he was bold enough to invoke in his polemic — though without breach of propriety — the name of the reputed mistress of the king, Madame de Cayla, whose influence was then considerable. His dexterity was so great that it was difficult to prosecute him. Later on, we have seen Prévost-Paradol likewise escape the clutches of a harsher and more formidable power than that of the Restoration. Their fates were similar: Prévost-Paradol's paper was suppressed, and Coste's review was bought up by the Villèle ministry.

This measure was neither skilful nor effective. A journal is not to be sold with its editors, like a plantation with its negroes. Nevertheless it was an annoyance; another field had to be sought for the young Liberals who were just fleshing their blades. "The young guard is beaten," said Thiers, already drawing his metaphors from that fertile source, the Empire. But the defeat was not serious, and the "Constitutionnel" retained a more formidable arm, or rather army. For that journal Thiers wrote in a style as easy, clear, and fascinating as ever, and perhaps more trenchant and polished than that of his other writings. He was not yet master of that propriety of political language, that art of disposing great masses of facts, that lucid and persuasive deduction, more cogent, perhaps, than the logic of correcter and more forcible writers, of which he has since produced so many models. But he treated political matters frankly, without invective or acrimony, overlooking puerile reproaches, and locking horns with the official spokesmen of the Government on the great questions at issue between aristocracy and democracy, emigration and patriotism, and above all, between the Restoration and the Revolution. Not all of his articles were direct political polemics; every subject gave opportunity for the expression of free and reasonable opinions as held by a man of flexible, clear, and serious intellect.

He even wrote for the "Globe" a series of articles on the Exhibition of Paintings, in 1822, — articles which were then collected and published in pamphlet form. He divined the strange genius of Delacroix and predicted the popularity of Horace Vernet, who made his *début* at that exhibition. Here is what he wrote of Gérard's picture representing Corinne inspired, which has been so often engraved: —

"The romance of 'Corinne' is thought to be the most fascinating work of a celebrated woman who astonished her century by the strength and vivacity of her organization, and especially by a boldness of thought foreign to her sex. Restless, impassioned, directed by the accident of her education toward lofty aims, Madame de Staël brought to these high intellectual regions all a woman's nature. Filling her books with warmth and with brilliant gleams of truth, she satisfied the multitude, which asks only to be moved and dazzled. But she never equalled the deep passion of Rousseau or the gentle passion of Bernardin de Saint-Pierre; she made everywhere attempts that were mistaken for results, missed the natural grace of the being that keeps its place, and was punished for not having kept her place, by want of charm, by disorder of mind, and by a celebrity whose burden the strongest man could scarcely bear.

"Madame de Staël's observations upon society are just and penetrating, — they prove her high intelligence; but her poetry is false. 'Delphine' seems to me, therefore, preferable to 'Corinne.' If, however, it is always best to be one's self, Madame de Staël should have reached perfection in 'Corinne,' which is the epic of herself. But she is here too much herself, surrenders too freely to all the excesses of her spirit. Yielding to that mystical German taste for what is just now termed the 'impressive' style, — which consists not in arousing sensations, but in eternally describing the sensations one feels, — Madame de Staël has succeeded no better than so many others in describing Italy; she has portrayed her impressions rather than the land that produced them. The ancients depicted things; Bernardin de

Saint-Pierre also depicted things, — they did not count their heart-beats one by one. And this is what gives their pictures such reality and life."

It is important to cite this passage, severe as it is, for Thiers would at no time have disavowed it. It was one of his peculiarities that he had no taste, or rather no esteem, for feminine genius. He had still less taste for the kind of literature that he here styles "impressif," — one of the few neologisms which escaped his pen, and for which he would have been more repentant than for the critique itself. Then, as later, Thiers entertained a very low opinion of the literature which consists in describing the impressions which things or ideas have made upon an author. His own method was to deal directly with things and ideas. He disliked and scarcely understood the subjectiveness, the psychological analysis, the scrutiny of sensations, which has been so greatly overdone during the last hundred years, and his distaste for declamation included the romantic and descriptive styles. No man was ever more unlike René, Faust, or Adolphe;[1] that dreamy spirit which, detaching itself from all personality, occupies itself with introspection and self-analysis, is of the North; M.

[1] Hero of Benjamin Constant's novel. — TR.

Thiers had all the clearness, security, and promptness of the Southern temperament. He knew no discouragement, no indecision, no regret for any course once taken. Of the two great families which divide the intellectual world, he belonged to the family of Voltaire, not to that of Rousseau.

This taste for simplicity, clearness, reality, pervaded his political articles in the "Constitutionnel." The Restoration school of journalists was a school of statesmen. The more philosophical school of the "Globe" and the more practical school of the "Constitutionnel" represented the two chief currents of the French Revolution. Notwithstanding recent paradoxical attempts to question the useful results of this Revolution, we may say that it established and aimed to realize three principles: First, the philosophic freedom of the human understanding, — the dearest wish of mankind from the time of the Renascence; next, the remoulding, in accordance with the principle of equality, of the mediæval social order which still existed ; finally, political liberty, under the only form then or now known, that of representative or parliamentary government. These three principles — freedom of thought, social equality, political liberty — were threatened at every moment by

the Restoration. There was no official public
defence of the first two, while the third, which
is the security for the two others, frequently
seemed to be endangered. These principles
were the horror of the clergy and the nobility,
and these bodies arrogated to themselves a
preponderant influence. The Catholicism of
that time, less inclined to legends and to ultramontanism than that of to-day, was more
counter-revolutionary, more distinctly absolutist. It was a religion of emigrants and of
courtiers. Almost without exception, defenders of the Church were enemies of freedom.
The nobility regretted the privileges of which
they had been so recently shorn. The Monarchy, especially under Charles X., would not
admit the permanence of the Charter, and
refused to regard it as the sanction of the work
of 1789. The presence of a Bourbon upon the
throne was to the Bourbon mind evidence
enough of the defeat of the Revolution. At
bottom, Charles X. had no more respect for
the Chambers than Louis XV. had for the
Parliament of Paris ; this was shown in 1830.

Even if they did not prepare a *coup d'état*,
the court, the king, and the Royalists thought
of it as a last resource which would be resisted
by none but the ambitious, the senseless, and
the designing, — for it is thus that partisans

characterize those who may be separated from them by some shade of opinion. What was the Ministry during the greater part of the Restoration, if not a party in power? Now, Thiers has somewhere said of a party in power that it is " a thunderbolt in the hands of a child."

The situation was a very critical one for all who desired the definitive triumph of the French Revolution, and every man had his own solution of the problem. Some, like M. de Lafayette, looked upon the case as decided, and thought that the conspiracy of the Monarchy against the Charter justified conspiracy of another kind. For M. de Lafayette any monarchy was, at bottom, merely a disagreeable concession which he might feel bound to make to his reason and to his country. None knew better than he the Old Régime and its miseries, which he had understood and condemned even if he had not himself been one of the sufferers. He recalled his youthful indignation when, as he was walking at Chavaniac, seeing the peasants kneeling to him as he passed, and kissing his hands, he said between his teeth : "Patience ! patience ! I must submit to it this once more, — but it is the last time." His suspicion was too well justified by his memory; and though he preferred the Bourbon Monarchy to the Empire, he cherished toward the Bourbons a distrustful repugnance. Public opinion having, however, accepted the legitimate king at the hands of foreigners, Lafayette had consented to what he regarded as a contract equally bind- ing upon the king and upon himself. Accord- ingly, when a reactionary ministry was formed, when the rumors of a *coup d'état* became con- tinual, he considered the contract void. And as there was for him but a step from thought to action, the moment he felt that he had a right to conspire, he conspired without reckon- ing the chances of success.

An old-fashioned party of this kind was cer- tainly the least dangerous of all to the Bourbon Monarchy; for rarely has an unorganized band of malcontents prevailed against the power and organization of a government. This party was scarcely represented in the press; in the Cham- ber it was represented only by M. de Lafayette, M. d'Argenson, and M. Manuel. It worked chiefly by means of secret societies composed of intrepid young men, among whom were some Bonapartists. Speaking of this party, Madame de Simiane, a stanch royalist, said to M. de Lafayette: "The honest men of your party have no superiors. Your *élite* is much better than ours, but our rank and file are as good as yours, and your scoundrels are worse than ours."

Another opposition was represented in the Tribune by M. Royer-Collard, M. Camille Jordan, M. de Serre sometimes, and Duke Victor de Broglie always. Their arms were more formidable than conspiracies: in the first place, oratory; then the "Globe" newspaper, which was edited by young men whose names still occur to every mind when one speaks of writers who have honored the vocation of journalism, — Vitet, Duchâtel, Dubois, Sainte-Beuve, Duvergier de Hauranne, de Rémusat. Feeling neither love nor hatred for the Restored Monarchy, these men contented themselves with expressing opinions of absolute liberalism in philosophy, in politics, in literature. All that they asked of the Monarchy was the application of these principles; and they accepted in advance any government, monarchy or republic, which would respect their opinions. It was not at all difficult to perceive that, of all governments, the one least capable of practising their theories was precisely the one which styled itself "legitimate," — that is to say, superior and anterior to every constitution, — but this inference from their writings they did not care to make explicit. M. de Broglie, who figured in the first rank among them, said in his "Memoirs" that they were "Revolutionists in ideas, Jacobins in meditations, applying to ideas the motto of the Revolution, ' Make way for me ! ' "[1] But in politics, as in Nature, opinions are represented by men, and systems by governments. From a revolution in opinion to a revolution in practice is but a step. The Emperor Napoleon was not mistaken in regarding theorists as dangerous. Yes, they are dangerous ; for they make men understand and hate tyranny, and point out to nations the safeguards of freedom ![2]

M. Thiers, by his very origin hostile to the Old Régime, almost a Bonapartist at college, prepossessed against clergy and aristocracy, had received his first political emotion from the spectacle of the double invasion of France and from the experience of the reaction of 1815 in the South. He brought to the Paris press the opinions of the French Revolution, whose cause he purposed resolutely to uphold, without hatred or wrath, without weakness or concession. His first articles in the "Constitutionnel" show that his opposition was founded upon the necessity of the case rather than upon the authority of principles. Never for a moment was he anarchical; from the outset his spirit of freedom was restrained by the

[1] Souvenirs du feu duc de Broglie, ii. 137.
[2] A page, dealing a little more in detail with the attitude of the Doctrinaire party, is here omitted. — Tr.

spirit of government. Less practically revolutionary than the deputies of the extreme Left, and less theoretically so than the writers for the "Globe," he had drawn from the Constituent Assembly, from the Convention, and from the Empire, a middle conclusion, — that of the necessity of a constitutional monarchy. But "he had a love for realities;" more than this, he had respect for facts. Taking counsel of history, he sought the type of this normal government where it in fact existed, — that is, in England, — and what he advocated was merely to shape the result of the French Revolution upon the model of the English. This was at bottom a new policy, although admiration for English liberty was then as now part of the Liberal tradition.

This policy he consistently supported, first in the "Constitutionnel," later in the "National," a paper which he founded after the failure, on account of minor differences, of a plan of union with the "Globe." The Doctrinaires, innovators in every field, were economists and romanticists. Already Thiers had his rooted dislike of free trade and of political economy, which he impertinently styled "wearisome literature."[1] But wherever he

---

[1] *La littérature ennuyeuse.* Carlyle's "dismal science" may be merely a free translation of this. — TR.

wrote, he appeared convinced that the cruel memories of the Revolution were too present to men's minds to admit the possibility of the Republic. He kept himself free from the illusions of Lafayette, while at the same time he feared lest the absolute principles of the Doctrinaires might bring about too radical a change of political organization. With a sagacity of which he was to give many a proof, he saw that the obstacle to freedom was neither the Charter, nor centralization, nor even the monarchical form; it was the principle of legitimacy. This principle concealed a power forever dangerous to the nation and its institutions; and a sovereign who should lay claim to no prior and superior right would give all the necessary pledges. Thus a revolution might be accomplished in a spirit of construction rather than of destruction. The thought was simple, strong, and nevertheless quite novel.

Such a government, founded on the ruins of the personal monarchy of divine right, must have a king who could accept and love the principles of the French Revolution, who should be sufficiently exalted in rank to have no rivals or equals, and sufficiently detached from the House of Bourbon never to unite with it. These qualifications could be actually recognized in a prince who stood upon the

3

steps of the throne. Without foreseeing that his accession would be the logical result of the political combinations of a young journalist from Provence, without in any way conspiring, this prince, taking counsel only of the memories of his family and of his youth, did nothing to render impossible the part he was to play. The Duke of Orleans, liberal, popular, in disgrace at court, was not an Emigrant, and had taken no part in the errors of the departure and the return of the royal house. He had served in the army of the Republic, and his father had given but too many pledges to the French Revolution.

These various circumstances tended to render the Revolution of 1830 acceptable to a public which is not very open to mere reasoning and theory. Nevertheless it was theory, — without which, said Royer-Collard, "it is impossible to know what we say when we speak, or what we do when we act"— that had guided Thiers in the choice of his opinion, and had brought him so near the standpoint of M. Guizot, who was to be so long his rival. The latter, without directly urging imitation, frequently cited the example of England. Thiers said very distinctly, "We must cross the Channel, not the Atlantic." In all his articles he supported a rational Orleanism; he threw all the flexibility and fertility of his mind upon the task of proving this the only practicable means of securing the triumph of the Revolution, and of terminating it, as it had begun, by the reality of parliamentary government. He advocated these principles for eight years with alternations of haste and patience, according as the ever-expected *coup d'état* seemed more or less imminent. Notwithstanding the great boldness of the thought, the expression was so carefully kept within bounds that he was never prosecuted, while M. Mignet, who afterward became so prudent, and the scrupulous M. Dubois, were condemned in the police court.

The general spirit of these articles does honor to the moderation and perspicacity of Thiers, and their result went beyond all' his hopes. It was a policy of reason formulated in anticipation of the mistakes of the government; its success required moderate revolutionists, bold conservatives, fearless liberals, a brave and wise people, a prudent and unprejudiced prince, statesmen of various parties uniting in a common work. And the astonishing thing about this policy is that it succeeded. A day came when King Charles X., who, according to the apt phrase of M. Molé, was "rather rash than resolute," gave the long expected if not long sought oppor-

tunity by conspiring against his own government, and thus made way for the pure Revolution of 1830.

Political writing did not exhaust Thiers'
activity. He wrote, for example, a biography
of Miss Bellamy of Covent Garden Theatre, an
article on Boisserée's book, one on Cologne
Cathedral, and a study of John Law, — the
first and almost the only article of a " Progressive Encyclopædia" which had been announced
with great parade. In an article on the memoirs of Marshal Gouvion Saint-Cyr[1] appears
the first trace of that taste for battles, and of
that talent for describing their fortunes, for
which he was afterward to be so famous. This
passage had the singular fate of being translated almost word for word by Mr. Disraeli,
and inserted without acknowledgment in his
panegyric on the Duke of Wellington. Moreover, M. Littré, with all his penetration, failed
to recognize Thiers in it, and printed it in his
edition of the works of Armand Carrel.[2] It
begins : —

" It would be difficult to persuade men, especially
those of a generation like ours, which has seen so
many soldiers, that of all the arts, the art of war gives

[1] Revue française, November, 1829, p. 196.
[2] Œuvres politiques et littéraires d'Armand Carrel, v. 132.

the greatest exercise to the mind. Nevertheless, this
is true; and the greatness of the art consists in the
fact that it demands character as well as intellect,
that it brings into play the entire man. In this
respect the art of governing is the only art which is
like it or equal to it. Consider, in fact, the works of
the most renowned poets, scholars, orators, — even
their finest works shall never reveal to you the temper of their souls. Consider, on the contrary, the
actions of generals and of statesmen, — invariably
you shall read in these actions the character as well
as the mind of the doer, for a man governs and a
man fights with his whole soul. Be it understood,
however, that governing does not here mean admin-
istering a province, and that fighting means more
than charging at the head of a regiment. Otherwise
this assertion would involve the ascription of mind
and soul to too many men."

It will be profitable to quote also an article
written in response to M. de Montlosier. M.
Sainte-Beuve has already printed it in his " Contemporary Portraits; " but how is it possible to
speak of the literature of this century without
following in the footsteps of this critic?

" No ! before '89 we had not all that we have since
had; for it would have been madness to rebel without motive, and a whole nation does not become in
a moment insane. Those concessions which you call
boons, and which I call restitutions, were extorted by

the Revolution alone. This one word recalls them all, and the contrasting word recalls the lack of them. Reflect that before '89 we had no annual representation, no right to vote taxes, no equality before the law, no eligibility to office. You maintain that all these things were in men's minds ; but the Revolution was required in order to realize them in laws.

"I can be as frank as you, and I admit that our party as well as yours is made up of men, and is moved by the passions of men ; the only difference between us is that of the justice of the cause. Among us, as among you, there may be vanities and wild passions ; plebeians born in our ranks might have made war upon the fatherland ; but you must concede, on the other hand, that nobles born in your ranks might have served in the Committee of Public Safety. We are all men, and our condition is hard. All parties have their good men and their bad men ; they differ only in aim. But you will agree that, between a Bailly dying with head and heart full of truths, and a d'Éprémesnil dying full of infatuation, although the sacrifice is the same the merit is not the same. Each died for his cause, but which one for the truth?"

This is the opinion of the French Revolution that Thiers expressed in his history, — a history which would alone suffice to give him a place among great writers. In four years (1823 to 1827), besides his other works and in spite of his youth, of which he must have had to hear much, he succeeded in publishing ten volumes, covering the history of France from 1789 to the 18th Brumaire. He had been obliged to associate with himself M. Bodin. This protecting name had been insisted upon by the publisher, who feared he would not be able to cover the expenses of the work, and who gained a fortune from it. After the third volume (1824), M. Bodin disappeared, and Thiers alone confronted the public judgment.

It was in fact a bold and serious enterprise, to relate, in the presence of those who had themselves been actors or sufferers, the story of a time so confused, so varied, so generous and so base, involving so many men and so many deeds. One might write the history of a whole century without finding so great a number of original characters to delineate and so many explanations to seek for doubtful actions. More than once the historian must have paused to ask himself what choice he would have made among the diverse factions of the time; more than once he must have perceived what his own experience afterward taught him, that in time of revolution the great difficulty is not always to do, but to know, one's duty. Moreover, the path had then been in no wise marked out. To-day we have at our disposal contemporary narratives, memoirs of all kinds, summaries which enable the mere schoolboy to form an opinion. At that time the historian had access only to the most impassioned testimonies bristling with apologies and recriminations; and witnesses in a court of justice, subject as they are to error and prejudice, are far superior to historical witnesses. He who first said: "I am not sure of this circumstance, for I have it from an eye-witness," was surely thinking of the spectator of a political occurrence. Contemporary history is merely a theme for declamation.

M. Thiers, who was in the course of his life to teach the French people many things which they have not wholly forgotten, began by teaching them the good they ought to think of their own history and of themselves. Was he cajoling them? Few critics said so then, and fewer still have thought so since. It has, however, been said, with some show of reason, that he lacked indignation against the crimes that stained the Revolution; and in such a case, to lack indignation would be to lack impartiality. The reproach would be just if it related to a dramatic history, such as Lamartine's "History of the Girondins," and the like. But Thiers' history is a simple narrative, the author of which does not profess to instruct

the reader what he should think. Nevertheless, it would be easy to cite more than one
page where misfortunes and errors are set
forth in a manner calculated to move the
reader. Who should feel the wounds inflicted
upon humanity and justice, if not those who
love the Revolution only for its generous origin and its beneficent results? It was the
Moderate party, the Liberal party, what is
called in the jargon of the Assembly the Left
Centre, — the party of which M. Thiers became the leader, — which suffered most from
that deviation from the principles of humanity
and justice during one of the periods of the
Revolution. Who, more than the Liberals, have
had reason to deplore the fact that two years
of the refined and just eighteenth century
should have deserved that sinister name, *the
Terror?* What stain of blood has this party,
save its own, shed in the cause? Was it not
the sufferer by all these crimes? While all
political factions in turn have invoked against
it these bloody memories as titles either to pity
or to admiration, it alone has always averted
its eyes from them with horror. To this day
we are the victims of this fatal inconsistency
of a nation which simply wished to raise itself
from bondage. At the end of a hundred
years the imaginations of men are still haunted

by the Terror: it renders some too timid to demand or to accept the freedom they long for; it renders others more impassioned for license, which is only one of the forms of oppression. The red flag in politics, like the purple rag brandished by the *torero* in the arena, serves at once as an excitant and as a bugbear. It is one of the most potent arguments of the enemies of freedom, right and left, and nothing is more fatal to the necessary balance of men's minds.

But though he is not insensible to the sufferings of humanity, Thiers takes much more pains to understand men than to judge them. He indulges in no paradoxes about the Jacobins, like those which M. de Lamartine, twenty-five years later, so inexcusably set forth with his splendid coloring. Thiers endeavors, not to justify them, but to touch the springs that moved them. "We find ourselves transported with him," wrote Sainte-Beuve, "to that dreadful mountain which we had beheld from a distance, veiled with storms and lurid with lightning; we ascend its cliffs, we explore it as we should an extinct volcano, and we come to understand that things could not have appeared from its summit as they appeared from below. Without clearing the guilty, we are led to account for them."

Thiers, like M. Mignet, is an impassioned partisan of the French Revolution; and for such writers private misfortunes are swallowed up in the greatness of the result. Thiers is like a general in battle, who cannot lament every wound because his eyes are fixed upon his aim, — victory. Individual conflicts, sufferings, death, seem inevitable, and he is led to something that resembles fatalism ; how can the historian quite guard against this? How resist the impulse to make one fact spring from another, to give to events and to men a more logical character than belongs to them, to deem their vicissitudes unavoidable? The better the story is told, the more that idea predominates, the less one perceives that events might have taken a different turn, or that it is possible to imagine a more probable course of things. It would be very convenient to think public misfortunes mere accidents, easily avoidable. But no; events must have taken place in such an order and in no other. If this impression be natural in a well-constructed narrative, how should Thiers escape the stumbling-block? In his purely narrative manner he frequently omits to draw conclusions; the reader is left to reason for himself, and to construct a philosophy of history as he goes along. The author is the victim of his extreme clearness, which exhibits facts in a bright light, and gives to all the character of evidence, of rigorous logic. But this logic is never used to justify excesses.

His style is original by dint of being simple. It is in some sense the style of Voltaire; but Voltaire, more elegant, sharpens his wit and makes it felt, while the satirical side in Thiers does not appear until later, in his speeches. In his history, the effort is to exhibit nothing except the facts. But the effort is not felt; these facts, so numerous, so complicated, show as through pellucid glass (the comparison is by Thiers himself), and not only facts and men, but all the details of administration and of modern war. Too frequently historians are thoroughly acquainted with only some features of their subject, and to these features they sacrifice the rest, concealing their embarrassment by suppositions or declamations. Here everything is in an equal light; by intelligent and assiduous labor the historian has mastered all the documents, all the State papers, all the negotiations at home and abroad. Not only was it the first time that the history of the Revolution had been written, it was the first time that life had thus been infused into historical writing. The author is not merely a historian, but a strategist, a financier, a statesman.

The style is so easy that one does not at first sight feel all its merit. It must be borne in mind that down to the present century, in France at least, history had been written only by literary men, who related it, as a pupil in rhetoric composes a Latin or a French discourse, without reality, without ever having lived, and without understanding what life is, in the world where the fates of empires are determined. Historians surveyed their subject from below, sometimes, in the case of superior minds, from above; but it is on a level with his subject that Thiers stands. In his " History of Charles XII." Voltaire had given historians a lesson, and had shown them that the scope of their subject has widened immensely, — that it requires more precision than formerly, more attention to customs, morals, law, commerce. But what a difference between a short and brilliant biography of a hero, and that entire world of writers, of orators, of generals, of stormy assemblies, which lives again on the pages of Thiers! As we read these pages, we feel that the robust intelligence of the author fits him not merely to relate the destinies of France, but to shape them.

When King Charles X. realized the gloomiest predictions of his enemies by issuing the Ordinances of July, 1830, he opened to Thiers

the career of the statesman. France replied
to the Ordinances by the triumphant insurrection which was so promptly appeased by the
organization of the Government of the Duke
of Orleans under the happily chosen name of
Louis Philippe, — a name recalling neither the
Louises nor the Charleses nor the Philips, and
severing at a single stroke the link between
the monarchy of the present and that of the
past.

CHAPTER II.

THE JULY GOVERNMENT.

THE Monarchy of July had no luck. In the first place it fell, — and to fall is always bad for a government, — and after its fall its principles were but feebly defended by those who had served it, and even by those who had founded it. Moreover, the later writers who have dealt with it have had their prepossessions, and have attacked it now from the conservative and again from the revolutionary standpoint. Like the Protestant religion, exposed to the anathemas of the Catholics against free investigation, and to the strictures of the critics who condemn that investigation as not being free enough, the revolutionary Monarchy has been fusiladed from every side.

Very few, in fact, ever loved the July Government in and for itself, and for the double reason that it was both the antithesis to the Restoration and the antithesis to Jacobinism. King Louis Philippe was one day complaining of his Prime Minister, M. Molé; and when his interlocutor replied that the minister was greatly attached to the Government, the king retorted: "Not so, for he is not before everything else an anti-legitimist." What defender of the Orleans Monarchy would speak thus to-day? After the fall of that fragile edifice it was natural that every one, according to his nature, should revert to his former faith, — some becoming Legitimists or Fusionists; others, who had no taste for the pomp and circumstance incident to monarchy, accepting or even seeking a republic. After 1848, M. Guizot, for example, could not fail to turn to the Right, M. Dufaure and M. de Tocqueville to the Left.

Those who were long inspired by the spirit of 1830 are rare. Rarer still are the publicists who have defended or even understood the constitutional theory of a government which had nothing of monarchy but the name, in which the national sovereignty was recognized, the king subject to the laws, and in which the casting vote belonged to the people. It must be admitted that this Monarchy, though based upon a revolution, is as legitimate as if it had descended in a direct line from Louis XIV. It is not a chance power, but a government with the same rights as others, and perhaps greater duties. One of the most distinguished historians of that epoch, M. Thureau-Dangin, has recently received the sanction of the French Academy. He is not absolutely an enemy; and yet the system that grew out of the Revolution of 1830 seems to him quite foreign and hateful. Of the government and of the personages of that time he has con- structed an image that has but little semblance to the reality. Whenever M. de Broglie or M. Guizot takes some liberal or popular meas- ure, he is ready to accuse them of weakness or apostasy. Whenever, on the other hand, M. Thiers signs a government bill or performs a conservative act, — an easy thing for him, — M. Thureau-Dangin takes care to remark that he is violating all his principles. He seems almost to regard Thiers as one of those bri- gands turned policemen by whom, according to M. Renan, social order was first founded. He fails to see that both classes were merely conforming to the consequences of the Revo- lution which had triumphed in July, 1830.

This is not all; the July Monarchy has suf- fered the further misfortune of being disliked, despised, traduced, by imaginative writers. And these writers are not without influence upon the opinions and especially upon the impressions of posterity. This Government based upon a philosophical theory, whose founders were men of letters, whose ministers were members of the academies, under which power was gained by literary and oratorical talent, in which men rose by intelligence alone, has been relentlessly scouted by those who owed their freedom of speech to the victims of their sarcasms. Except Casimir Delavigne, Scribe, and Alfred de Musset, all the writers of the time — Balzac, George Sand, Frédéric Soulié, Eugène Sue, Charles de Bernard, Lamartine, — affected to scoff at the *bourgeois* Government which aimed to give power to merit alone. Victor Hugo himself, although a peer of France, did but tardy justice to it when, much later, he drew a just portrait of King Louis Philippe in "Les Misérables."

The cause of this strange aberration of literary sentiment is far to seek. It might be supposed that young lords of the Old Régime or socialistic workingmen are the only men capable of fascinating the artless heroines of Balzac and of George Sand. This, however, is not necessarily true. M. Sardou has given the Engineer an enviable place in his novels and comedies; and this Engineer may be justly suspected of entertaining Republican sentiments, without ceasing to be loved. In judging these writers we must take into account their natural disposition to carp. Literature adheres to its traditional attacks upon power, even when that power has itself become literary. Perhaps when statesmen had no longer any claim to power save that of being men of intellect, rivalry necessarily arose. Down to the French Revolution there had been a gulf between men of letters and statesmen. The former looked up from beneath to the masters of the world, whom they made no attempt to equal or even to rival. Modern society grants power on the same conditions as literary fame; it would seem that letters had been dignified, but literary men have preferred to believe the contrary. It is a weakness of human nature that it does not greatly respect what it does not fear; that this weakness tends to disappear, is a fact which does honor to our time. But, to take the case of a very excellent and fair-minded man of letters, it is not improbable that M. Mérimée bore more easily the heavy yoke of an emperor's nephew and of an inglorious minister chosen by the favor of the master, than he had borne the authority, liberal as it was, of one of his confrères of the Academy, who had no claim to power save that of having written the History of Civilization, or the History of the Consulate, — works whose style is inferior to that of " The Etruscan Vase."

Thus the July Revolution, which was in-

tended to establish the reign of reason, — and
what is more intellectual than that? — became
a target for the raillery of the new literature.
Under the Restoration the purely literary men,
whether vaudeville-writers or novelists, from
M. Étienne to M. de Chateaubriand, made
every effort to transform themselves into journalists, and the first ambition of every one
who could hold a pen was to write a political pamphlet. The new generation took an
opposite course. Weariness, the need of innovation, the scepticism that treads upon the
heels of revolutions, the unexampled development of the imagination, — a faculty that had
been long benumbed in France, — all contributed to make men seek in the art of
writing the forms and the effects of style. The
theories of art for art's sake led young men to
think that literature has no aim beyond itself,
and that it is the privilege of talent to repudiate
its debt to ideas. The most beautiful phrase
was to be that which contained the least
meaning. Every one knows what dexterity
Théophile Gautier displayed in this game.
Accordingly, it was deemed original and convenient to exclude from the Republic of
Letters all who made a useful application of
their art, especially those who employed it in
writing or speaking upon politics, — above all

the moderate, liberal politics for which artists of all classes expressed their contempt by the term *bourgeois.*

It must, however, be admitted that if the men of letters could not pardon the Government for giving them the freedom for which they should have been eager, the politicians repaid them with an equal disdain. The late Duke of Broglie characterized the literature of his time as "toad's broth." One of the first journalists of our age, M. John Lemoinne, has related that during the Insurrection of 1871 M. Thiers asked him one day concerning M. de Sacy. "He is growing old in peace," was the reply, "consoling himself for present evils by reading the classics." "Ah! he is quite right," cried M. Thiers; "Romanticism is the Commune!"

The month of July, 1830, presented to the world the noble spectacle of a nation sure of its position, revolting against arbitrary authority, awakening against it, to cite the famous words of the Duke of Broglie, "that delicate and dreadful right which slumbers at the feet of all human institutions as their sad and final safeguard." The still blood-stained people of Paris contented themselves with a moderate solution, which was in entire harmony with the national opinion. According to some sages of to-day this moderation was the effect of fear. France was like a boy who, having climbed too high, clings to a branch that he may not fall and perish. On the contrary, it was like a squadron which has been ordered to occupy a given position, and which takes and holds that position. The bold and reasonable spirit of Thiers seems to have presided over these events. We know by many witnesses how great was the part he played; it was he who went to Neuilly to bring back the Duke of Orleans. But before relating the last act, the first must not be forgotten, — the protest of the journalists which inaugurated this Revolution.

In the office of the "National," St. Mark Street, was held a meeting of writers, who were more immediately affected than other citizens by the July Ordinances, for the purpose of considering, not armed resistance, which was not anticipated, but a protest the form of which was still to be determined. M. Léon Pillet, editor of the "Journal de Paris," proposed to draw up a collective protest which those might sign who would. This proposition being eagerly accepted, M. Thiers, with Messrs. Chatelain, Cauchois-Lemaire, and Rémusat, was selected to write the paper, but it was Thiers who composed the whole of it. This is not the only opportunity he had to protest against arbitrary acts or infringements of the national sovereignty. It is interesting to see how well he measured the force of his style with the gravity of the deed, and to compare this memorial with his words nearly fifty years later, apropos of the 16th of May, 1877. But the times were very different. In 1830 matters were very serious, and M. de Broglie said on that very evening to one of the signers, thinking him not sufficiently alive to his danger, "Do not be deceived; those people will be extremely cruel."

For Thiers this manifesto marks the transition from the career of the journalist to that of the statesman, from the article to the action. Before he spoke in the Chamber he published a pamphlet[1] defending the Revolution and the resultant Monarchy. This brochure sets forth the principles of the new Constitution as publicists had beforehand explained them and as the friends of this Monarchy accepted them. In order to understand the July Government, we must bear in mind the conflict between different classes of its friends, — between those who had heartily favored Louis Philippe and those who had merely accepted the situation,

[1] La Monarchie de 1830, par A. Thiers, député des Bouches-du-Rhône. 8vo, Paris. A. Mesnier, 1831.

as in a shipwreck one takes the first frail bark
that comes along. The one class, whose chief
care was to keep intact the party of progress,
desired to make the Revolution bring forth an
abundant harvest of freedom and reform; the
others attached themselves to the past, and
sought to make good their alliance with the
friends of the Old Régime. During the first
years the difference was not very obvious, both
parties being occupied in defending the menaced social order; but the dissension was to
develop into open hostility.

Never have circumstances appeared better
suited to satisfy philosophers and to throw
light upon an exposition of the doctrines of
constitutional law. The example of resorting
to force in order to change institutions, without valid motive, without wise reflection, had
been set by the Bourbon Government itself, so
that the favorable rôle of resistance had fallen
to society. But reasonable and gentle as this
resistance was, it was a revolution, — the swift
work of passion and force; and both in passion
and in force there is a danger difficult to suppress. Their greatest danger lies in the fact
that they offer a spectacle which disturbs the
conscience and the reason. It was to re-estab-
lish tranquillity in France, to show the people
their victory, and to teach them not to abuse it,

that Thiers' pamphlet aimed. After a revolution the statesman has to deal with three classes of people: first, those who regret the past simply because it is the past; secondly, those who wish to profit by circumstances to carry the movement beyond its legitimate results; finally, the class—not the least dangerous nor the least numerous—who are frightened by the movement after having themselves encouraged it. This reaction of fear is the most formidable of all; we have encountered it more than once in the course of this century.

It would be going beyond the scope of this very intelligent and practical brochure to inquire how far the Government of 1830, or the succeeding Republic, was capable of fulfilling the wishes which the French people have entertained for the past hundred years. Both the Charter and the Constitution of 1875, with the difference of an intervening half-century and of universal suffrage, have realized what the French Revolution could not accomplish, but made possible. The failure of that Revolution was due solely to its sins against humanity, justice, and liberty, and all its lessons are favorable to the liberal policy. The conclusion must ever be that society and government, being human inventions, are subject to the great law of human affairs, and that politics is therefore governed by morality. In politics the relations of deed and law, passion and reason, are the same as elsewhere, and nothing is right that is not *right*, just that is not *just*. Now under absolute power, whether it be that of the Old Régime or of modern dictatorship, human nature is never intact and pure, absolute power acting necessarily by intimidation or corruption. It is political freedom alone that leaves man his moral freedom; it alone can serve as the corner-stone of legitimate authority, and the art of constitutions is to make reason prevail and to get it freely acknowledged.

Under the Restoration, Thiers, being in 1830 but thirty-three years old, would have been obliged to wait seven years longer before he could become a deputy; but the legal age was lowered by the new Constitution. Even before his election, in 1830, by the Electoral College of Aix, he took part in the deliberations of the Assembly in the capacity of Under-Secretary of State in the Finance Ministry, a post which he held under two successive ministers, — M. Louis and M. Laffitte. Before he had actually spoken, his method was familiar, the second of these Ministers having read from the Tribune expositions of financial policy which were by Thiers, and which, by their sagacity and simplicity, had pleased the House. His friends were therefore not so anxious about what he might say, as about his manner. His enemies noted his short stature, his bearing, his eyes hidden behind his spectacles, his Southern accent, which, however, soon wore off as his voice became intense and animated. For it must be admitted that he had enemies. Even then he had to suffer from the injustice of public opinion, from the violence of the press, from the ill-will of those who dislike new-comers or who fear rivals, from the contemptuous aversion of men of affairs for men of letters whose intelligence alone makes them politicians.

It was his enemies who were pleased by his first two speeches on finance in the autumn of 1830. He spoke with monotonous diffuseness, with hesitating and incorrect copiousness, and seemed incapable of effectively repelling the insults of the opposition journals. Never was a *début* more deceptive. The Ministry was disliked by the deputies, who overwhelmed it with attacks of all sorts. It appeared to them — though the idea now seems very exaggerated to a reader of these speeches — that Thiers was trying to imitate the Girondins and the orators of the Mountain, and that, having through his historical studies become familiarized with Mirabeau, he had some ambition to resemble that Revolutionary orator. Distant as was the imitation, the effect of it was bad. In political assemblies it is dangerous to imitate any one. Of all kinds of oratory, parliamentary eloquence is that which demands the most absolute sincerity and naturalness. A man may write otherwise than as he thinks or speaks, creating in himself an artificial talent which may be bold in a timid person, sentimental in a hard and selfish person. Even a preacher in the pulpit, a lawyer at the bar, may, without offending, speak with an impassioned violence which contrasts strongly with his ordinary sluggishness; but before the House a man must appear as he is. One may certainly be a declaimer like M. Berryer, if declamation be, as in him, a second nature. M. Guizot was bound to express himself from the Tribune after the fashion of a doctrinaire professor, M. de Lamartine as a harmonious poet. In order to succeed, it was necessary that Thiers should hit upon a tone thoroughly in keeping with his person, his voice, his talent. The simplest borrowed phrase rings false from the Tribune. The Chambers are full of distinguished men who have broken down as speakers for want of having struck the key suited to their personality.

A few months after this partial check M.

Thiers had happily triumphed, not only over his physical difficulties, but over the contempt and prejudice with which his maiden efforts were greeted. His first success was in the dis-cussion of the Address to the throne, shortly after the accession to power of M. Casimir Périer (March 13, 1831). The Périer Ministry was completely in harmony with the principles of the late Revolution; what distinguished it from the preceding administrations was the firmness with which these principles were sup-ported. Force and decision succeeded weak-ness and shuffling indecision. This change was certainly not of a character to displease Thiers, who was nevertheless embarrassed by the obligation of defending at times the Min-istry in which he had served. This he did, notably in reply to M. Humann, who in an exposition of the state of the treasury had been very aggressive. It was on this occasion that Thiers made his celebrated complaint against " the art of grouping figures."

He was also somewhat distrustful of M. Casi-mir Périer, fearing lest the outspoken language of this minister might provoke a European war. It is well known how the great powers treated the Government of the House of Orleans. Metternich's Memoirs, unkind as they are, give but a faint idea of it; for the prince, hostile as he was to France, to constitutionalism, to liberalism, to all the *isms*, as he called them, had received the Revolution with the equanimity of a man who has foretold an event, who is dissatisfied with those who have rendered it inevitable, and who does not suffer from it himself.

The other conservative powers were more threatening, and the anxiety arising from this cause delayed Thiers' adhesion to a Ministry which appealed to him in so many ways. At last his confidence in the wisdom of the king, in the firmness of General Sebastiani, Minister of Foreign Affairs, in the good-will of England, and especially his own reflections (for ideas seldom came to him from without), all united to banish his distrust, and in the debate of August, 1831, he made a speech on foreign affairs which was an event. Its merit was enhanced by its unexpectedness. The members of the former House could not believe that this was the same man whom they had condemned to silence for the rest of his life. The speech has indeed some faults, but it shows also his best qualities, — order, clearness, precision, the art of making everything accessible, tangible, decisive. Its somewhat incorrect eloquence is animated by a warmth and a feeling which impart even to common-

places something of the originality of the
speaker. It was at once perceived that he
would rival Guizot as a master of the Tribune.
Some years older than Thiers, Guizot had
spoken in the last parliament of the Restoration, and had likewise rapidly recovered
himself after a first attempt which had fallen
short of the hopes of the admirers of his great
mind, his noble features, and his sonorous
voice. It was certainly not by the last two
qualities that Thiers distinguished himself; in
fact, it is perhaps impossible to give an idea
of him to those who have never heard him.
There is in the orator's art something that
must escape posterity, and for this very reason
it is just that we should not be chary of our
admiration for speeches which, even without
the personal magic of the speaker and the
responsive thrill of the audience, remain good
and useful works. All speeches, even those
of Thiers, gain by the author's delivery. His
half-hidden gray eyes would flash with profound shrewdness, while his set features and
his short hair made him resemble certain Roman busts to which energy and intelligence
lend a kind of beauty. Grand ideas, deep
sentiments, transfigured his countenance, his
accent became graver, and then his head would
assume a noble attitude. One may say, with-

out a paradox, that although his figure, his face, his bearing, his voice, were all unpromising, none of them was an embarrassment to him even in the Tribune.

Thiers became Minister of the Interior in the Cabinet of the 11th of October, 1832, under the presidency of Marshal Soult, the Duke of Broglie being Minister of Foreign Affairs. A month later Thiers was selected to explain the policy of the Cabinet, and this new success seemed greater than the former. The speech began with one of those rapid summaries of the history of France since the French Revolution, — summaries which he was so often to repeat with such truth and variety that his hearers never wearied of them. Space fails wherein to cite even fragments, as also to enumerate and discuss the changes of ministries with which parliamentary governments are so often reproached, and which constitute one of their inevitable drawbacks. The enumeration of them can be read in the histories of the epoch, and still better in the short prefaces which M. Calmon has supplied to each of the speeches published by him. They form an excellent history and a convenient running commentary. This commentary and these speeches bear witness to the immense activity of a mind able to master and elucidate not only questions of government, but those of finance, of war, of administration. Like the great English ministers, Walpole, Pitt, Robert Peel, Thiers could grapple with all subjects and could speak of business affairs as well as of politics. In the treatment of every subject he exhibited the same attractive lucidity, the same solidity of discussion, all the marks of technical knowledge and thorough competence, without a trace of pedantry.

His faults must also be mentioned, for the sake of completeness. His copiousness sometimes runs over into prolixity, and his simple manner now and then borders upon vulgarity. His arguments are not always as strong as they seem plausible. He sometimes mistakes clearness for evidence, overstates his case, under-estimates the validity of objections. He takes too much satisfaction in instructing, but it must be admitted that he never fatigues. Like Voltaire, he has been accused of being superficial. Neither he nor Voltaire has much regard for ideas that cannot be popularized; that is, grasped by the unaided power of common-sense. Like Voltaire, also, he was little inclined to innovation, and when he erred it was never on the side of rashness. Strangely enough, his timidity in the matter of reform was most marked when he was in opposition.

In power his boldness was greater, and in this his was truly an executive talent, for he did not dread responsibility. He would take a course that he would not have ventured theoretically to advise.

In action he took his course boldly, provided he had time to reflect, — for his mind, keen as it was, was a little slow in grasping new ideas. One might say that he was at once bold and timid, temporizing and urgent. In ordinary times the companions of his struggles complained of his delays, of his hesitation, of the difficulty of getting him to sacrifice his tastes or even his pleasures, of his repugnance to entering into combinations which he had not devised. But the moment he saw a political necessity, he gave up everything, — rest, health, work; his weariless activity begrudged nothing; and when his mind was made up, his somewhat solitary fashion of thinking and acting independently of others gave him singular strength and confidence. He knew neither discouragement nor doubt. Thus if all his qualities had their reverse side, his faults had their good side. So it is with superior men ; and in describing such a man one is tempted to recall the scene in Molière's " Bourgeois Gentilhomme," [1] wherein Covielle sets forth the

[1] Act iii. Scene 9. M. de Rémusat makes some judicious omissions. — TR.

defects of Lucile, while Cléonte, affecting to
agree, suggests the corresponding merit: —

"*Covielle.* To begin with, her eyes are small.

Cléonte. Yes, it is true, but they are full of fire, the
most sparkling, the most searching in the world.

Covielle. As to her figure, she is not tall.

Cléonte. No, but she is well shaped.

Covielle. She affects a certain carelessness in her
speech and actions.

Cléonte. True, but all that is becoming to her, and
her manners are engaging, — they have an indescrib-
able charm that fascinates the heart.

Covielle. As to her intelligence —

Cléonte. Ah, Covielle ! her intelligence is most refined and delicate.

Covielle. Her conversation —

Cléonte. Her conversation is charming."

This last applies even better than the rest to
M. Thiers, whose conversation has been much
praised. To tell the truth, it was not precisely
a conversation, but rather a fluent monologue,
full of sallies, anecdotes, historical parallels.
It was very much like one of his speeches;
indeed it often was the speech itself, or a fragment of the speech, which he was about to
pronounce. It exhibited the talent of composition, one of the best gifts of the orator; he
would follow a logical deduction for a whole
evening throughout interruptions of all kinds,

returning to it after the most unforeseen and the most prolonged digressions. Here, as in the House, he paid slight heed to objections, his own ideas appearing so clear to him that those of others remained a little obscure. He seemed not to hear them at the time; but it was not unusual to see him return of his own accord to an idea which he had at first rejected. He needed to wait until an idea, deposited in his brain, had germinated in the particular form which his own ideas assumed. So his friends seldom interrupted him, and this not only out of deference, but because it was useless; they found compensation in the charm of his facile, copious talk, full of fire without declamation, of unstudied grace, of unpretending images.

Thus it was, at least, in the last twenty years of his life; and M. Doudan tells us in one of his letters[1] that we should have found him the same in early life.

Paris, April 10, 1840.

M. Thiers dined here on Monday. He talked of Africa with a vivacity that charmed Albert, among others, saying that it gives us the only instinct in the least disinterested or heroic that remains to our country; pointing to the Atlas Mountains as a kind

---

[1] Mélanges et lettres de M. Doudan, i. 307, 308.

of military school where all the officers of our army are inured to danger, to vigilance, to presence of mind; proving from all his military souvenirs that there can be no better soldiers than those who have served against the light-horse. He made us see the Arabs galloping down the African hillsides, and the unyielding French infantry scattering that mountain-storm with its regular fire. And then the memories of the Army of Egypt, the curved sabres and turbans of the Mamelukes, the names of Heliopolis and of the Pyramids, and the fray between the Roman Legion and the Numidian horsemen. M. d'Haubersart seemed not in the least moved by all this, and persisted, in spite of the Numidians, in spite of the days of Heliopolis and Tabor, in reckoning upon his fingers how many soldiers we had in Africa, how many we had lost within ten years by fever, how many on the road to Constantine and to Mascara. And M. Thiers, with a kind of Gallic frenzy, led against him all the invincible armies trained in Africa, with their beautiful tattered battle-flags waving in that dazzling sunshine, and all the noble company of heroes bred in war; and still M. Duvergier insisted that it was a very expensive military school. . . . M. de Canouville listened in silence to all this tumult, and after the departure of the President of the Council he said to me: "It's very odd; I am not of his opinion, but this little man reminds me of the emperor's manner and vivacity of speech on the days when he was not quite reasonable."

Nothing could be more lifelike than this picture, except the last touch, which is evidently inserted for effect; for M. Doudan, a great enemy of the Empire, and M. de Canouville, formerly the emperor's quartermaster-general, knew very well what Napoleon was like when he was "not quite reasonable." Apropos of Algeria a characteristic anecdote used to be told. Its conquest dated back to the Restoration, and was completed after the Revolution of 1830. Of course there was a discussion whether we should not abandon it, as we are accustomed to do whenever a colony has been gained by dint of some hardship and heroism. The ministers decided that it must be retained. "It is a school of patience," remarked M. Guizot. "It is a school of war," retorted M. Thiers. "At all events, it is a school," concluded M. de Broglie.

As to the analogy between Thiers and the Emperor Napoleon, one can scarcely imagine any except their common vivacity, their sensitiveness to impressions and their power of forcibly rendering these impressions, their inexhaustible, imaginative improvisation, their sometimes blind irritation against obstacles, — all characteristics of Voltaire also; for it is by their defects that the spoiled children of genius and fortune resemble one another. Napoleon had a certain conformity with Thiers in his way of looking at great social institutions, — the clergy, the university, administration, the courts, commerce. On all these points Thiers' manner of interpreting the Revolution differed little from that of the First Consul; it was by an effort of mind and by his clear view of practical needs that Thiers became a defender of a free press and of parliamentary government. To put it differently, he did not precisely love freedom, — there is the analogy; but he loved a free constitution, — there is the difference.

But let us return to the eloquence of Thiers. He left little to the intelligence of his hearers, and did not fail to repeat his arguments and to explain by the card the origin and the history of every question. This fault was so agreeably hit off in a famous novel of that time, that we must quote a page of it. Jerome Paturot, who has become a deputy, is telling his own story:[1] —

"There was another orator of the first rank, and him I took as my model. I could not enough admire his rapid rise. In order to conquer a great place in the House, he had had to contend against

---

[1] Jérôme Paturot à la recherche d'une position sociale, par Louis Reybaud. Paris, 18mo, 1842.

physical obstacles, — his voice, his stature, his insignificant appearance. The men of brilliant success in the Tribune had the advantage of him in these respects. He had overcome these difficulties by dexterity of speech, by fertility of resources, by flexibility of talent. He was my idol, the master of my choice. Whenever he climbed the marble staircase of the Tribune, I pulled myself together, like one who is about to receive a lesson. I must do him the justice to say that he was not niggardly of his lessons ; he gave me all the time I needed to imbue myself with his manner and inspire myself with his method. What especially pleased me in him was that he began with the rudiments of every question, which he did not leave until he had exhausted it. He always took it for granted — Heaven knows how justly ! — that the House was ignorant of the very alphabet of things ; this showed a profound study of the human heart. Thanks to him, I came within an ace of understanding the Eastern question ; one speech more, and I should have grasped the problem. Unhappily I stopped short with a four hours' lesson. This was too little ; but what I know of the subject I owe to the orator who was my star. Through his efforts I learned that there is upon the Bosphorus a city named Constantinople, where the Turks are in the majority. It will hardly be denied that this is a notion very essential to any lasting solution of the Eastern question. A few lessons more, and I should have learned something about Egypt and Syria, countries famous in antiquity."

This method of teaching — of sacrificing
everything to clearness, of impressing the
hearer by sheer force of fact and argument,
of holding the whole attention in order to
convince — often impelled Thiers to assume
the incorrect tone of conversation; but what
seems like negligence was sometimes an arti-
fice. When he was not addressing the Jerome
Paturots of his time, he could change his tone,
and recollect that he was a great writer as well
as a popular orator. On the 20th of June,
1833, while still in office, he was elected a
member of the French Academy. Out of
twenty-five votes his competitor, Charles Nodier, obtained six, and there were two white
balls. On the 13th of the following December M. Thiers was received by M. Viennet.
After having spoken with taste and measure
of the youth and early works of Andrieux,
whose place he took, and then of those pretty
tales and comedies, which would now be
thought a little insipid, the new academician
took an opportunity to make the customary
survey of the age in which his predecessor
had lived : —

" What times, what things, what men, between that
memorable year 1789 and that no less memorable
year 1830 ! The ancient French society of the
eighteenth century, so refined but so ill-regulated,

ends amid a dreadful storm. A crown falls by violence, dragging down the august head that wore it.
Likewise, and without reprieve, fall the most precious
and the most illustrious heads; genius, youth, heroism are victims of the wrath of factions, embittered
by all that is delightful to men. Out of this bloody
chaos suddenly rises an extraordinary genius who
seizes this society with his powerful hands, gives it
stability, gives it glory, gives it civil equality, — the
most pressing of its needs, — postpones the freedom
which would have been but an embarrassment, and
bears to all parts of the world the prevailing truths
of the French Revolution. One day his tricolor
banner flashes upon the heights of Mount Tabor, another day upon the Tagus, a last day upon the Borys-
thenes. And then he falls, leaving the world full of
his labors, the human mind full of his image. The
most active of mortals goes to die of inaction upon
an island of the great ocean !

"Such, gentlemen, are the grandeurs we have
witnessed. Whatever be our age, many of us have
seen a part, some of us have seen all. When, in
our childhood, we were taught the annals of the
world, they talked to us of the storms of the an-
tique forum, of the proscriptions of Sulla, of the
tragic death of Tully; they repeated the stories of
unhappy kings, of the misfortunes of Charles I., of
the blindness of James II., of the prudence of William III.; they told us also of the genius of great
captains, of Alexander, of Cæsar, until, fascinated by
the tale of their greatness, we wished that we might

have seen with our own eyes those potent and immortal men.

"Gentlemen, our eyes have really seen, our hands have really touched, all these things and these men. We have seen as bloody a forum as that of Rome ; we have seen the heads of orators displayed from the Tribune whence they had spoken; we have seen kings as unhappy as Charles I., more miserably blind than James II. ; we behold every day the prudence of William ; and we have seen Cæsar, Cæsar himself ! Among you who hear me are men who have had the honor to approach him, to meet his flashing eye, to hear his voice, to receive orders from his mouth, and to fly to execute them amid the smoke of battle."

M. Guizot, so long his rival, was elected the next year. Starting from very different points, and very different in their methods of reasoning, these two thinkers had arrived at the same practical conclusion, — the engrafting of the English government upon French society. During the foundation period when this government had to be defended from subversive attacks, their agreement was almost complete. Fatal consequences have been attributed to their later disunion, just as the causes of that disunion have been sought in a rivalry of talents and influence, in a mean jealousy, in all those lower human sentiments to which they were strangers. Both of them were very early convinced that they had no need to be jealous of any one.[1]

The greatest enemy of the July Government was M. Berryer. M. Thiers said of him that this definition of oratory should have been invented for his benefit,— " It is a body speaking to a body; " and added: " With my voice and figure I need truth on my side; I succeed only with truth, while Berryer is the orator of falsehood." At that time the saying was very just; but later, under the Empire, M. Berryer showed that he also knew how to plead for the truth. He had the good fortune to end his days as member of an opposition which, according to M. Thiers, was right at all points,— a rare thing for oppositions, for governments, or for humanity.

In the time of Louis Philippe the case was different, especially the case of M. Berryer, who was the spokesman of an opposition wrong at all points, since it was bound to be at once Legitimist and Liberal, to attack and insult not merely conspiracies, but the natural defence of an oppressed nation, and, in the

[1] A long quotation at this point, from a eulogy upon eloquence, pronounced by the author's father on the occasion of the reception of Jules Favre to the French Academy, is spared the reader. There is mention in it of several orators, but of neither Thiers nor Guizot, though they seem to be referred to with discreet academical allusiveness. — TR.

name of princes enthroned by foreign hands, to accuse of weakness abroad a government that had just raised the tricolor flag. More than once he drew upon himself a bitter response from Thiers, who on these occasions seemed to borrow weapons from his adversary. Any one who takes the trouble to read over his speeches of December 31, 1834, and of January 22, 1835, will find that Thiers knew how to forsake the tone of racy conversation, and to rise to a more classical form of eloquence. For example, he said to the Royalists : —

"Legitimacy ! What security did it give us? Reflect : it thrice permitted the legitimate throne to fall. Was Louis XVI. not legitimate? Was Louis XVIII. not legitimate? Was Charles X. not so? But a single breath of Revolution sufficed, in 1789, in 1815, in 1830, to overthrow their legitimate throne. Such is the security that you promise us. What then is this power which thrice failed to save its own throne, letting it fall before the first popular breath? If this is your boasted security, away with you ; for to have faith in it we had need forget the history of our own time. . . . Security you could not give, for you fell thrice ; clemency? you shed blood and denied the prayers of mothers ; dignity? you put yourselves into the keeping of strangers. How can you ask the country to expect anything from that principle of legitimacy which was able to assure it against no storm, which gave it neither security, nor clemency, nor dignity?"

It is a pity to be forced to confine one's self to a few short quotations, since one of the beauties of his speeches is their simple and excellent arrangement. Enough has perhaps been quoted to show his ability to cope with M. Berryer, even when the latter had the choice of ground and weapons. And yet Berryer was the most perfectly gifted of men for that oratorical action which the ancients valued so highly. His open and expressive countenance, his broad chest, his powerful voice, his bearing at once noble and animated, that precious gift of remaining natural in the midst of declamation, of working up a passion without apparent art, of hiding a great deal of shrewdness under a frank exterior, made it impossible to forget him once one had heard him, even when he was enfeebled with age.

The years when the Government of the House of Orleans had to defend itself only against revolutionists — Radicals as we say to-day, Carlists as they were then called — was not precisely a golden age, for blood too frequently flowed in the streets; nevertheless, it was an era very honorable to the nation and to its chiefs. It was the easy moment of a

government, when it is still supported by all
the forces that have created it, when the party of
the past has not yet plucked up courage, and
when what calls itself the party of the future
has not yet begun to hope. On either hand
there is a period of expectation, and it is then
the duty of the founders to do all they can to
confirm the freedom and the strength which
they have gained. Then it is logical that di-
vision should arise. Government is not an
end in itself, but a means either of accomplish-
ing reforms or simply of furthering the public
weal; and as soon as the Monarchy appeared
settled, it was inevitable that the counter-
currents of conservatism and liberalism should
begin to flow.

An incident contributed to delay this inevitable moment. For reasons that cannot
be given here, the king had been led, after
various trials, to call M. Molé to the presidency of the Council,[1] and to form the Ministry of the 15th of April, 1837, — a strange
Ministry which satisfied nobody, in which sat
none of " the princes of the Tribune, the grand
vassals of representative government " (the
expression is Sainte-Beuve's). Solely by reason of its origin and composition, this Cabi-

---

[1] Molé succeeded Thiers on the 6th of September, 1836.
Guizot went into opposition on the 15th of April, 1837. — TR.

net had formidable enemies. Under the representative system a ministry of this kind is reduced to impotence, and can have no higher ambition than merely to prolong its own existence. This is, however, not enough; and many people are found, especially outside of the ministry, who fail to see the necessity for its existence, and who make that existence difficult. Opposed from every side, M. Molé made it a point of honor to maintain himself in power. Not being a great speaker, he was obliged, in order to.succeed, to endeavor to postpone the discussion of important questions; to win if not to corrupt individuals; to scatter discord in political parties; in short, to bring to bear upon the Assembly the diplomacy of the conclave. Such a course seriously detracts from the advantages of parliamentary government; and it was natural that those who were attached to this form of government should be dissatisfied, and that, separated as they were by shades of opinion, they should be drawn into union. Hence the Coalition.

Nothing would have been more legitimate, had party chiefs not taken advantage of the situation to exaggerate their grievances, and had they preserved an attitude of sufficient moderation toward a government which they did not wish to overthrow, but simply to warn.

This is a delicate art, wherein our parliamentary leaders have often failed; their failure in it contributed to bring about the Revolution of 1848. Our liberty was not, perhaps is not yet, the robust freedom of England. Parliamentary wranglers should not forget that they are before a public which may be tempted to treat them with no more consideration than they show for one another. This caution was especially important in the time of restricted suffrage. Notwithstanding all the respect inspired by the name of Guizot, it must be admitted that in this struggle he was the hottest and the most abusive. He has expressed his regrets for this in a page of his Memoirs.[1]

Thiers did not at once associate himself with the Coalition, of which Guizot was the head. Either through a sentiment of moderation, or because he felt that the opinions of Minister Molé were little more at variance with his own than those of Guizot were coming to be, he for some time refrained from any attack upon the Ministry. In January, 1839, however, when the Address was up for discussion, he rose like the rest to enumerate his grievances against M. Molé; and it must be admitted that Thiers had only too good reason to reproach the Minister with his timidity, his inaction

---

[1] Mémoires pour servir à l'histoire de mon temps, iv. 287.

through fear of taking any risks, his exclusive concern for material interests, and with his foreign policy, which led him to abandon Spain, to neglect England, and to evacuate Ancona.

It is certain that this debate was a serious blow to parliamentary government. As at the end of the first act of Victor Hugo's drama the lords successively reproach Lucrezia Borgia with all her crimes, so here each party chief, Guizot, Thiers, Berryer, Barrot, one after another ascended the Tribune to enumerate, with evident exaggeration, the faults of the Government. The public took them at their word, and passed judgment, at once severely and unjustly, upon the régime and upon the king himself, whom they had imprudently exposed. Minister Molé's opinions could not be popular, but he sustained the unequal struggle with so much grace and dignity that people took pity upon him, and a certain discredit fell upon the alliance of men of talent who so bitterly attacked him. Guizot had closed one of his speeches by applying to courtiers this phrase of Tacitus: *Omnia serviliter pro dominatione.* M. Molé immediately began his reply with the words: "Tacitus said that not of courtiers but of the ambitious." And even in the House the success was with the Minister.

Ambitious! Was Thiers ambitious? It is

an insult to a public man to say that he is not
so in a certain degree; it implies that he has
too little confidence in his ideas to desire to
apply them. Thiers certainly wished to realize his ideas, nor did he distrust his own ade-
quacy to the task. But he did not love power
for itself, nor even for the pleasure of commanding, nor yet for the importance that it
confers. With little eagerness for advancement,
jealous of his freedom and of his leisure, he
often desired power in order to act; but he
could not keep it long, precisely because
he wielded it to some purpose. He loved
only his favorite pursuits, and often took a dislike to affairs for which he felt no special in-
clination. Even as President of the Republic
he was very sincere in his willingness to resign,
and very eager to regain the freedom of his
time and of his tastes.

In these somewhat tumultuous debates of
1839, Thiers took his permanent stand as the
defender of all progress compatible with the
July Government, while Guizot became the undisputed leader of the timorous conservatives.
Henceforward there were in France Whigs and
Tories ready to contend for influence, if not
for the ministry. At bottom, the difference
was not very great, and need not be so. Both
were Liberals, devoted to the Monarchy of

1830; but while the one endeavored to conciliate those whom the late Revolution had
offended, the other undertook to satisfy and to
unite the deputies and the electors who were
more exacting in the matters of democracy
and reform. Not that Guizot was absolutely
hostile to reforms ; his superior mind admitted,
understood them all ; but he believed that they
could be carried out by none except conservatives. All his speeches during those eighteen years are eloquent variations of this theme.
He lauded repose, wealth, peace, timidity in
everything, confidence in governmental initiative. He showed extreme art in concealing
the background of distrust, fear, scepticism,
which disfigured this policy. He said one day
that M. Odilon Barrot displayed great talent
in " putting breeches [*culottes*] upon opinions
that wanted them ; " it might have been said
of Guizot that he was accustomed to drape
with the toga opinions which had only a
citizen's costume.

Thiers' repugnance to novelties was so well
known that he has been taxed with under-
valuing the usefulness of railways. The accusation is quite baseless ; notwithstanding
some things which he let drop in conversation,
it was in fact during his ministry that the
first railroad bills were passed. In foreign

politics, in electoral reform, in everything, he was more inclined to a bold policy than Guizot. Thiers thought, in flat opposition to his rival, that a conservative policy should be carried out by Liberals, and that men of the most advanced opinions should be intrusted with power. The separation of the two policies and of the two men was brought about by the Cabinet of the 1st of March, 1840. The formation of this Ministry was a difficult task, for Thiers found himself at the mercy of a disaffected conservative party, and of a dissatisfied liberal party. It was, however, with reference to Eastern affairs rather than to domestic policy that the dissent betrayed itself. The question was not one of choice between war and peace, but of judging how far boldness might go without becoming rashness. Thiers was Minister of Foreign Affairs, and Guizot his Ambassador to England. The latter, like the king and the Chamber, deemed the game too hazardous. It may have been so; if fifty years ago the question was hard to answer, how much more difficult would it be to-day! What sacrifices could Europe be asked to make? To what extent could a monarchy improvised by a popular insurrection impose its will? The Crimean War proved that Russia was not invincible, and this glorious war was fought by the army of the Monarchy, — the army organized by the generals in Africa and by the princes of Orleans, who must not be forgotten when we speak of the good that was done between 1830 and 1848. But the condition of Europe was less alarming in 1855 than in 1840, and the war which succeeded at the later date, though without great advantage to France, might have failed had it been undertaken sooner. It was this question that brought about the fall of Thiers and the formation of the Guizot Ministry (October 29, 1840), which was to lead from the Monarchy to the Republic.

Thiers and his friends were thrown into an opposition which was certainly not a factious one. Their criticisms, rarely bitter, were softened by the sincerest declarations of respect for the Constitution. Their speeches are models of constitutional opposition, though it may be difficult to believe this, so frankly revolutionary have opposition parties calling themselves moderate since become. As to the numerous points at issue between the Opposition and the Government, it would be irksome to recount them. But there were two questions which this constitutional Opposition had especially at heart, and which drew from the National Guard the cry, "Vive la ré-

forme ! " — a cry so far from being revolutionary that it is the safeguard of free governments
when they listen to it in time.

The reform in question comprised two modifications of the state of things brought about
by the Revolution of 1830, — the extension of
the suffrage, and the diminution of the number
of office-holders in the Chamber of Deputies.
In 1830 the amount of the assessment that
every citizen had to pay in order to exercise
the right of suffrage had been reduced. In
view of the spread of education and intelligence
its further reduction now became natural and
necessary. A still simpler method of extend-
ing the foundations of our free institutions appeared in the proposal to convert the exercise
of one of the liberal professions into an electoral qualification. Strangely enough, under
a government claiming to be in the hands of
the middle class (*la bourgeoisie*), neither law-
yers nor physicians, the very flower of the
French middle class, were admitted to the
suffrage. To accede to such a proposition
would seem an easy and an honorable way to
satisfy an opposition party. Yet in resistance
to this, Minister Guizot delivered one of his
most admirable speeches (March 26, 1847),
insisting upon the deep gulf that separates
intelligence and capacity.

The effect of parliamentary reform, the grounds for which seemed peremptory, would have been equally prompt. It was proposed, not to forbid every office-holder to be a deputy, but to limit the number of office-holders in the Chamber, of which a clear majority were Councillors of State, Attorneys of the king, Justices of the Royal Court. Here was a manifest abuse, an official tie that appeared to diminish the authority of the votes of the Chamber. Independence of fortune or position does not, indeed, guarantee men from all weakness. An anecdote was in those days current of the reply made by a very rich lord to a poor deputy who had reproached him with some compliant vote: "It is very easy for you to quarrel with the Administration; but suppose, like myself, you had ten thousand acres of woodland!" When, in 1863, Thiers entered the Corps Législatif, Guizot remarked to much the same effect: "Ah! M. Thiers used to complain of a Chamber of office-holders; he will now find out what it is to deal with a Chamber of proprietors." But under the Empire, the manner in which the deputies were elected was the regrettable thing, and the imperial Corps Législatif can be compared to no other parliamentary body. It defies comparison! For all that, the composition of the

Chamber furnished a pretext for pointing out the abuses of parliamentary government, and it is difficult to cry out upon the abuses of a thing without somewhat discrediting the thing itself. In avoiding this last difficulty, however, Thiers and his friends displayed admirable talent, and a moderation that would be disputed only by the blindest adversaries; and M. Odilon Barrot maintained a similar attitude. The reforms then urged by the extreme Left were of a narrower compass than the liberties of Englishmen, and did not go beyond what had been taught by the publicists of the' Restoration period. Harmony was really, therefore, no impossible thing between the liberal leaders of a conservative party and so conservative an opposition.

Perhaps the foregoing remarks sufficiently explain why this harmony was not brought about. Another reason worthy of note seems to have escaped attention. The conservative leaders, M. Guizot, M. Duchâtel, M. Vitet, were a hundred-fold more disposed to concession than their party; and to grant what was asked for would have necessitated on their part an effort as difficult and as meritorious as that which Sir Robert Peel was making at about the same time in England. They were not mistaken in thinking that a part of the

Chambers, and even of the country, was growing alienated from the purely liberal spirit in
which the Revolution had been carried out
and the government founded. Peace and the
accompanying growth in wealth, which was
favored by wise laws and an enlightened administration, left to a considerable fraction of
the middle class no interests save purely material ones. Doubts, suspicions, fears of all
kinds, were gradually taking possession of the
reactionary party, and this party pushed the
Government toward timidity and distrust of
reform, — toward the side, to quote Guizot's
own words, "on which governments fall." At
a time when it was necessary to be enterpris-
ing and bold, to counteract both the turbulent
agitation of hostile parties and the apathy of
friends by means of a fruitful activity, the
Ministry seemed disposed to set up a half-
hearted prudence as a political theory. They
retreated even from the positions they had
taken. A law concerning secondary instruction defended by Messrs. de Broglie, Cousin,
Villemain, and Guizot, had been passed in
1844 by the Chamber of Peers. An excellent
report upon it was laid before the Chamber of
Deputies by Thiers. But the Ministry dared
not accept its discussion, for the reason that
it was too favorable to the University, too un-

clerical. Not that alone: the University, whose
members were and are the best supports of
freedom and the rule of reason, was oppressed
and humbled. It was thought thus to win over
the clergy and the Legitimists. This weakness did not prevent them from illuminating
their Faubourg St. Germain on the evening of
the 24th of February, 1848, nor did it make
M. de Montalembert one whit the less implaca-
ble in his war upon the Government.[1]

Finally, in the elections between the years
1842 and 1845, the composition of the majority of the Chamber was considerably modified
and by no means improved. New deputies
appeared, whom it must have been surprising
to find among the supporters of a government
the chief defect of which was that, by reason
of its origin and the character of its founders,
it was too prone to treat men as pure intelli-
gences. In order to appreciate this, we must
return to the literature of the period. As we
have seen, literature had exhibited an impassioned hostility to this government by men of
letters. Nor is this all: a famous author en-
dowed with a creative faculty whose power has
perhaps never been equalled, being out of con-
ceit with the virtuous political society of his

---

[1] An invective quoted from Montalembert is here omitted. — Tr.

time, conceived the plan of creating a society to his own taste, if not in his own image. With marvellous relief, reality, and life, he painted a fantastic world filled with all sorts of people, whose sole thought is to give themselves the greatest sum of pleasures, of amours, and of money, and who employ to these ends all the resources and all the facilities of power. This imaginary world stood in no relation to the living world. The heroes of Balzac were very different men from the publicists, the historians, the orators, who discussed in the Assembly and disputed the power from 1830 — or even from 1815 — to 1848. In order to find politicians like Balzac's we should be obliged to go back to the time of Louis XV., and to Louis XV. himself, — for even his ministers had opinions, and for them pleasures were the privilege of power, not its aim. These novels were nevertheless so fascinating, the author's talent, realistic in everything save the general conception, was so superior, the public mind was so perverted, that people were found who took this imaginary society as their model. Literature was no longer the portraiture of society, but society began to pattern after the fictions of literature. Then it was that there arose in the Chamber a race of young, audacious men for whom politics was merely another field for jobbery, for gambling, or for amusement. Fortunately none of them attained to power under the July Monarchy; their hopes were not to be fulfilled until some years afterward. But this mock aristocracy, this foam upon the surface of the middle class, — an aristocracy which, according to a saying of the time, " had not, like the ancient nobility, conquered the Gauls, had not, like the imperial nobility, conquered Europe," which, borrowing from the society of the past the spirit of frivolity, and from modern society the spirit of calculation, entered upon politics not to acquire seriousness but to win the delights of sensuality and of vanity, — contributed to give to the final years of the Orleans Monarchy the unfortunate character that its enemies would attribute to the whole régime. Needless to say, men of this species have no place in the liberal ranks. They are the forlorn hope of the conservative party.

This has taken us very far from Thiers, who did not read Balzac, and was totally unlike Maxime de Trailles. His taste inclined him to give no heed to the unjust accusations against the majority, which were incessantly repeated. He had himself been so often slandered that he was loath to believe anything of this kind. He confined himself to the policy of defending the principles of 1830 in speeches on the University, the Jesuits, the Budget, and on the subject of reform. Do these speeches show an unfailing grasp of the situation? Certainly his opinions, had they been carried out, would have given a new lease of life to the Monarchy. But he seems to have been blind to an obscure movement of the time, an anxious, vague expectancy, a confused but widely penetrative feeling that political reforms were of less importance than a social revolution. He did not, however, carry this illusory confidence so far as M. de Barante, who wrote, in the Address to the king from the Chamber of Peers, thirty days before the catastrophe:

"Opinions subversive of social order and detestable souvenirs have agitated rather than perturbed the public mind. Such agitations are powerless against the social order. Yes, Sire, the union of the great powers of the State, the action of law and of public reason, will suffice to preserve the repose of the country."

Nor would he have written as did Guizot to Prince Metternich (May 18, 1847) : —

"France is now favorable to the policy of conservation. She has long since reached her goal and taken her footing. Many oscillations yet, but weaker and shorter, like those of a pendulum swinging to a halt. No profound and turbulent fermentation with respect either to home or to foreign affairs. There are at present two counter-currents in France, — one at the surface, and apparently still revolutionary; the other below, and in reality strongly conservative. The deeper current will prevail."

But although they had too much confidence in the solidity of the Monarchy, neither Thiers nor his friends would have anything to do with the campaign of banquets. This well-known movement was to reveal the rash imprudence of some, the no less imprudent confidence of others, and the brittleness of the Constitution. Toward the close of the year 1847 the Ministry had declared that the meetings, or banquets, held by the candidates were illegal, and that they could be interfered with, even when held in a private house. Nothing would have been easier than to reduce the dispute to the dimensions of an interpellation, and to leave the decision to the Chamber. Instead of this, the Government hit upon the device of proposing an opposition banquet at Paris, — the same Paris where no review of the National Guard had been ventured for seven years. This banquet was to be broken up by a police officer, and the matter was to be carried before the courts. Few governments could with impunity assume such a risk at such a time. Had

the proposal emanated from the Opposition, it
would have looked like a trap. But no! The
Opposition, even the Republican wing led by
M. Odilon Barrot, lent themselves to the scheme
with repugnance.

To this scheme Thiers was frankly hostile.
Although rather irritated than alarmed, he
thought such a demonstration would be useless to the cause of reform, and that it would
present a favorable opportunity for insurrection, or at least for disturbances. The Government, even if not shaken, would then have a
pretext for an energetic appeal to the solici-
tude of conservatives. Such is the attitude of
the moderate party on occasions of this kind:
it is to overshoot the mark, to permit one's
attacks upon a government to arouse the fears
of the friends of the social order. Abuses of
freedom have done less harm by stimulating
the audacity of extremists than by exciting the
dread of the indifferent.

Thiers' apprehension was much increased by
a secret incident of which he latterly sometimes spoke. He often received anonymous
letters, especially from an unknown correspondent whose advice had always seemed
to him judicious. On the 21st or 22d of
February, 1848, he found, on his return to
his house, a long and able letter from this

correspondent, reproaching him with his careless confidence, his inactivity. The situation was graver than he thought; we were nearing the crisis of a great democratic movement to which he ought to ally himself; he would do better to commit himself, to compromise himself a little, were it only for the purpose of moderating and guiding the movement, of making it more innocent and more useful; he was losing time in the gratification of his artistic and social tastes, and was limiting his political activity to mere conversations with Rémusat,[1] that *ermine* who, for fear of soiling his fine robes, would meddle with nothing. This letter impressed Thiers, and he remarked that very evening to the man whom he was reproached with listening to, " It may be that we must resign ourselves, every fifteen years, to see democracy make some great forward stride." Nevertheless, he was inclined to regard the demonstration then in preparation as too insignificant to be dangerous. This was his disposition with respect to affairs in which he took no part. "Take care," he had said to some of the ringleaders, " if you miss the chance to make yourselves odious, not to miss the chance to make yourselves ridiculous."

[1] François Marie Charles, Comte de Rémusat (1797–1875), father of Paul. — TR.

He, however, warned the Ministers, but they thought that the demonstration would be a pitiful failure, that the masses would take no interest in it, and that the Opposition would be weakened by it.

Those who favored the movement persisted in expecting a demonstration which, without seriously disturbing the peace, should exhibit the state of public opinion in so formidable a way that the Ministry would be forced to retire. The Ministry indeed fell, and the Monarchy with it. Thiers, who was summoned only the night before the king's flight, had not time to take a single measure or to sign an order; the decree making him Minister was not even written. He had hardly time to advise the king to leave Paris without abdicating, and to await the event at a distance at the head of faithful troops. But it was too late to carry out or even to discuss the plan which, twenty-three years later, was to save the Republic. Thiers could only witness, with a sinking heart, the flight of the king whom he had served, a democratic Revolution which he had done everything to avert, and the rise of a new power that was more than all else to transform the conditions of government in France, — universal suffrage.

CHAPTER III.

THE moralist is bound to think that the February Revolution lacked two things: a great cause and a sufficient grievance. When force is the only recourse against injustice, when the weight of the complaints equals the gravity of the enterprise, not only revolution but sometimes murderous conspiracy is absolved by history. It does not appear that the present case is one of those which justify an act blamable in itself. The July Monarchy, if not "the best of republics," was nevertheless really a very habitable republic, moderate, open to reform, and capable of being made more liberal and more democratic every day. It was to the public interest that progress should go forward slowly, and that we should not pass at a bound from a too restricted electoral body to a nation of voters. The Republic, based upon universal suffrage and so soon to be threatened by it, arose among a people poorly prepared for self-government, and greatly surprised by what had been forced upon them by the Parisians. This restless population of Paris, always ready for the fiery defence of an idea or of a man, without scrutinizing too closely the value and the seriousness of the idea or of the man, had also been somewhat surprised by this easy victory. The obscure but real socialist movement was scarcely apparent outside the circle of secret societies and professional revolutionists. Very few deputies, perhaps few ministers, had read the works of Fourier, of Saint-Simon, of Considérant, which disturbed the imaginations of the simple at a time when more positive minds were inflamed by Lamartine's " Girondins."

The fundamental opinions of Thiers and his friends were such that they could hardly have had any absolute repugnance for the Republic. What they had desired from their youth up was a balanced government, wherein the casting weight should belong to the nation. They could not believe with the extreme Right that the Republic meant universal ruin, nor with the extreme Left that monarchy could exist only by the humiliation of the masses. The Duke of Broglie, M. Duvergier de Hauranne, and many others, have often declared that liberal France may choose between a republic which borders upon constitutional monarchy, and a monarchy which is a republic in everything but name. Political liberty, that is, the participation of the people in their own government, is better subserved by a republic than by legitimate monarchy. In one of his last speeches in the Chamber (February 2, 1848), Thiers had gone even beyond these principles : —

" I am no Radical, gentlemen ; the Radicals know this very well, — one has but to read their journals to be convinced. But understand me well : I am of the party of the Revolution, both in France and in Europe. I wish the government of the Revolution to remain in the hands of moderate men, and shall do what in me lies to keep it in such hands. But even if this government passes into the hands of men less moderate than myself and my friends, into the hands of passionate men, even of the Radicals themselves, I shall not on this account abandon the cause ; I shall always belong to the party of the Revolution."

These sentiments were shared by the majority of the men who had labored to establish the July Government. They objected to the Republic merely because they perceived the difficulty of making it permanent; indeed, their absolute want of faith in the conventional traditions upon which are based the majesty and the very existence of monarchy inclined them to accept the Republic. Such was the feeling of moderate Opposition deputies like M. Dufaure and M. de Tocqueville. The latter, having studied democratic government in the only country where it existed, had early broken with the Legitimate Monarchy to which his family was attached, and had at no time shown any confidence in the July Monarchy.

But Thiers was no mere theorist; he was also a man of feeling and a statesman. His conduct was rarely guided by absolute principles; the affections and personal impressions always materially influenced his decisions. How could he witness without emotion the flight of the king whom he had loved? How could he help regretting the Monarchy which he had created in his mind, founded with his own hands, what though it had perished for not heeding his counsels? Had he not defended this Government as the only safeguard against the return of the heirs of Charles X., and against the dangerous dreamers who wished to go beyond the revolutionary monarchy? He had always advocated a middle government, that should satisfy not only what Guizot called the "governing classes," not only what Odilon Barrot called "the people," but the *nation;* and in explaining these words to the Chamber of Deputies one day, Thiers produced at once an article for a dictionary of politics and a profession of faith. Bérard, in his "Course in Physiology," explains that between muscular inertia and violent contraction there is a peculiar muscular state which he calls the force of "fixed situation." This force was displayed by Milo of Crotona when he pressed a pomegranate in his palm, so gently as not to crush it, yet so powerfully that no one could force his hand open. Thiers' opinions show some analogy with this force exerted to preserve. In 1848 the pomegranate was not crushed, but the protection invented by doctrinaires for freedom and society was injured. The hand had been violently opened, and the delicate fruits of civilization were endangered. Thiers, as a politician, was never insensible to the spectacle of force; perhaps he was somewhat over-impressed by it, and his first impulse would be either to take possession of it or to resist it. This latter impulse first seized him upon the advent of universal suffrage, and controlled his conduct throughout the following years.

The first care of all good citizens was the maintenance of peace. To those who under the Monarchy had dreaded the cruel extremity of war, it seemed that a democratic revolution must revive the fears, excite the wrath, and rally the forces of all the absolutist parties in

Europe. The Provisional Government and all serious politicians were haunted by spectral coalitions. This fear of war had the good effect of rallying military men round the banner of a Revolution which they disliked, because it had been for them a kind of defeat. Happily these apprehensions were not to be realized, and justice must be done to M. de Lamartine. Between lyric democracy and monarchy done into heroics, there was no room in his soul for the epic; military glory found him very disdainful.

But there were solider pledges of peace. Liberal England had her grievances against the Guizot Ministry, and hastened to give the Republic the benefit of the principle of non-intervention. The Emperor of Russia was too great a partisan of the Old Régime to anathematize a revolution that had dethroned a usurper and had exiled the worst enemies of legitimate monarchy. There was every indication that he would be more indulgent to the Republic than he had been to the Orleans Government. The Pope had been compelled to promise the Romans a constitution. There was an insurrection at Milan, a victorious uprising at Berlin, the Republic was proclaimed at Venice, and Metternich, the inveterate enemy of the House of Orleans and of France, had fled to cover. Peace was assured, and with a little more boldness and presence of mind the Provisional Government might have turned the situation to better account. The February revolution, by heartening the peoples and disheartening the kings, had totally changed the European status.

Reassured on this head, Thiers resolved to devote himself to the rescue of the nation from social perils. This he could do only by entering the Legislative Assembly, which was to be elected on the 19th of April. He was not sanguine with respect to this future Assembly, and was disposed to think that he would be relegated to a Girondin minority destitute either of influence or of authority. He drew this inference from the general state of men's minds, from the course of the Government, from that perversion of reason often produced by revolutions in those who make them, as well as in those who suffer them. Thiers had at first refused a candidature at Marseilles, the success of which appeared equally improbable and undesirable; afterward he consented, and here is the letter he wrote to a friend: —

PARIS, March 3, 1848.

I had hoped for a while that my electors of Bouches-du-Rhône would relieve me from standing. I counted upon the clergy to reject me. I am but

half reassured, and I still fear to be elected, notwithstanding my circular, which has had, I freely confess
to you, a very great effect. No speech of mine has
been so favorably received.

I am very sorry that I did not refuse the seat from
the outset. I take a dark view of things. For this
I have good reasons, too long to relate. I am dis-
gusted with things without exception, with men with
very few exceptions, and I dream only of a lodging
in a little house at Rome. Should I be fortunate
enough to escape election in Bouches-du-Rhône, my
mind is made up ; I shall renounce the living world,
and pass the remnant of my life in a corner, laboring
— at what ? At the history of the world, which has
been my dream from childhood. I shall not write it,
but I shall have the pleasure of studying it. Thus
I shall have more men to include in my sweeping
judgment. Verily there must be something behind
the screen whereon the events of this world are
painted ; otherwise the mockery would be too great.
They say freedom is triumphant to-day, and here we
are almost proscribed for having defended our Government against itself. Such is justice !

M. Thiers failed without regret at the general election, but he did not carry out his
plan of retirement. Both he and the electors
changed their minds, and on the 8th of June he
offered himself to five constituencies at once.
He was returned everywhere, even from Paris,
where he was placed upon an oddly matched

ticket alongside of General Changarnier, and of Messrs. Victor Hugo, Pierre Leroux, Caussidière, and Louis Bonaparte.

As he was walking to the Chamber for the first time, one of the loungers of the Place de la Concorde accosted him, as is usual on such occasions, with, " Whatever you do, don't give us America ! " To which Thiers made the sensible retort: " If you won't have North America, mind you don't get South America !" It is between these two Americas that France had, and still has, to choose.

Thiers got himself put on the Finance Committee, where there seemed likely to be less prejudice against his advice than in the purely political committees. The elections had turned in favor of moderate counsels, and the Constituent Assembly was very prudent. Perhaps he saw the danger too exclusively on the financial and economical side. He and his friends reproached the last ministers of the Monarchy for having had eyes only for the reactionary movement, and they themselves suffered an opposite illusion of the same kind. The events of February made the hitherto somewhat limited reaction much more marked, and, so long as political rights were not imperilled, Thiers favored it. Until the practical demonstration of this peril by the conspiracies of

Prince Louis Bonaparte in 1851, Thiers remained the most impassioned of Conservatives, taking this much abused word in its best sense.

One of his great services to this cause was his "Defence of Property,"[1] published in September, 1848. The book is amusing, clear, copious, a bit superficial, and the only very original thing about it is the author. The reader is constantly drawn on by the attraction of a strong and lively individuality. How is it possible to reflect that the ideas are not very new when they are so evidently new to the writer, who sets them forth by the unborrowed light of his own mind? He has the conviction of a man who has been at the pains to discover his ideas, and who makes even commonplaces his own. He does not dream of inquiring into the metaphysical principle of the right of property; yet it does not appear that the more technical philosophers who plume themselves upon their rigorous accuracy have ever seen in it anything more than a consequence of human freedom, or rather freedom itself in one of its forms, — in short, a necessity of civilized society. Is this not solid ground upon which to base a right? Thiers develops this thought in his usual spirited

[1] De la Propriété, par A. Thiers. 8vo, Paris, 1848.

way, dwelling upon nothing which is not accessible to mere common-sense. His own common-sense was a keenly whetted instrument, a weapon most effective against dangerous Utopias. In a speech of the 6th of May, 1834, he had said of it: —

" A statesman should be possessed of good sense, a primary political quality ; and its fortunate possessor needs a second quality, — the courage to show that he has it. What I am saying is widely applicable to the times in which we live. People of good sense are not lacking ; the quality is not so rare, since it goes by the name of *common* sense. What we lack, is men who dare prove their possession of it."

This courage and good sense were never less lacking to Thiers than on the occasion when he refuted Socialistic theories by the report of a committee appointed to examine Proudhon's propositions concerning the reorganization of taxation, public credit, mortgage loans, paper money, and the right to labor.[1] Here Thiers shows his mastery of that attractive and convincing method, in which he has never been excelled, of bringing practical truths home to the minds of an Assembly always prone to inattention. It is well known how easily he triumphed over his antagonist

[1] Report of July 26, Speeches of August 2, September 13, October 10, 1848.

in a Chamber which had been elected under the influence of the February gale. M. Proudhon, who seems to have been neither a thoughtful seeker after truth nor an inflexible sectary, but rather a writer for effect, a retailer of paradoxes, found but one person (M. Greppo) to share his defeat.

The slight support which the enemies of society found in the Republican Assembly, and the less easy victory of General Cavaignac over the bloody Insurrection of June, 1848, ought to have convinced the public that the greatest danger was over, and that our disease was not so desperate as to warrant a desperate cure. But, as has happened more than once in human history, the peril averted by the eloquence of some and by the heroism of others began to appear greater, once it had been encountered. Memory seems to be more timid than Imagination. After having victoriously defended itself, society began to look about for a savior. Moreover, the name of Bonaparte had come up at the May elections (1848), and throughout the first half of the century that name retained a magical power. When it was spoken, the nation seemed unable to listen to reason. What a series of misfortunes and mistakes have been required in order to break its spell! Prince Louis Bonaparte, elected in several departments, gave and took back his resignation several times, got himself re-elected by the most various constituencies, surrounded himself with several outcasts from fortune and from politics, succeeded in inspiring so much faith in his duplicity that nobody believed his Republican protestations, — played, in short, the part of a pretender. He became the most serious rival of General Cavaignac, whose candidacy seemed to be proclaimed by events, and whose great heart was worthy of such a fortune. M. Ledru-Rollin figured as the representative of the Socialists and the Jacobins.

The greater number of Thiers' political friends, Messrs. Dufaure, de Tocqueville, de Lasteyrie, de Rémusat, declared for General Cavaignac. Without foreseeing the extreme consequences of the success of the rival candidate, they distrusted that predestined race; and their foresight, which was perhaps as instinctive as the enthusiasm of the masses, attached them to the Republic. Thiers, on the other hand, believed that the French people were at that time little disposed to accept a master. Of the two chief preoccupations of the statesman, order and freedom, the latter seemed to him assured; he was more inclined to fear anarchy than despotism. He hesitated long, however, for the reputation of the Boulogne and Strasburg conspirator was not precisely such as to inspire confidence. Finally, he made up his mind to vote for the Prince. He thought that a supreme interest commanded all good citizens to unite in defence of the social order, and that the establishment of the Republic would take away both the desire and the power of stirring up a new revolution. He was to make the same attempt later on, under conditions more tragic, and, in some respects, more favorable. But now, not believing in the success either of General Cavaignac or of the Prince of Joinville, he wished to strengthen the conservative party with the popular power represented by the name of Bonaparte. As the prince in whom this power was invested had been the hero of no expedition to Egypt, of no Italian campaign, there was some chance that he would not be found altogether infatuated, and deaf to good advice. His election was certain, and it might seem imprudent to array the friends of social order against the national will.

Thiers represented at that moment an important section of public opinion, which he did much to mould and restrain. He reassured and held in check the once liberal middle class, which was then inclined to sacrifice

its principles to an exaggerated need of security, and to push conservatism to absolutism,
Catholicism to Ultramontanism. M. de Falloux
has published interesting "Memoirs," which
recall a memorable personality and a Machia-
vellism that is not without its artlessness. He
seems to wonder that Thiers did not fear the
social peril so much as to rally to the House
of Bourbon. What an aberration of party
spirit! Apart from the fact that such an
amende honorable would have been a sacrifice
such as Thiers could hardly have made with
dignity, no reason appears why he should
have been expected to make it. He was seeking some force to set against the roaring tide
of demagogy. He could find points of support in a parliament, in eloquence, in well-
considered laws, in modifications of universal
suffrage, in the name of Bonaparte, in the
magistracy, the clergy, the army. But the
claim to reign by hereditary right over a people that had so often denied the right, — what
could it be but a source of weakness to a government? It was important to make broad
the forehead of resistance, and M. Falloux and
his friends proposed to restrict it to the narrow
regal fillet. They would have appealed to all
citizens, not in the name of order and of conservative principles, but in the name of the

8

Count of Chambord, in the name of a principle constantly rejected, in the name of a flag that had long been a symbol of defeat. How many honest men would not have given over the defence, had they not felt that in fighting for order they were fighting for the Republican order!

Prince Louis Bonaparte's success went beyond all anticipations. Less than a year after the fall of parliamentary government in the most delicate of its forms, after an appeal so direct and unreserved to the national will, the Chief Magistracy became lodged in the hands of a representative of the unlimited power of a single man. The popularity of a name, the witchcraft of distant memories, the perpetual illusion of the Monarchists, the coalition of the discontented, the hopes of the outcast, — all had combined to give unexpected strength to the anti-Liberal movement. The mark was certainly overshot, and the new Chamber soon aggravated the situation. The Constituent Assembly had won distinction for its courage, its good sense, its honesty. It was one of the best legislatures that France has had. In the Legislative Assembly that succeeded it, the moderate party hardly existed; the Republic was represented only by a scarped and rugged Mountain. The more or less conservative majority was made up of dismissed

officials, of disappointed politicians, of demoral-
ized Liberals, of angry capitalists, of confident
Legitimists, of Bonapartists who were already
almost conspirators. These partners of a day
would have sacrificed everything to the double
purpose of resisting the Reds and of reacting
against the February Revolution.

Thiers' first speech in this Assembly, which
was to live so brief a span and to die so op-
portunely, had but one aim,— peace. The
Revolution, which had acted upon France as a
narcotic, had acted as a stimulant abroad, and
the name of Bonaparte was not calculated to
allay uneasiness. In June, 1849, Thiers accordingly rose to defend the Government's Italian
policy and to favor the credits for the Roman
expedition. This action was a considerable
pledge to the conservative opinion of Europe,
— a pledge that cost Thiers little, for he had
always been favorable to the Holy See and
even to the temporal power. "What next,
now that the Pope plays the Liberal?" Metternich was saying at about this time. But
what so irritated Metternich, made it easier for
the French Liberals to come to an understanding with the Catholics. As to the temporal
power, Thiers had more than once advanced
the ingenious and very disputable opinion that
if it be true that nations have the right of self-

government, this right was not infringed in the
case of the Romans. The States which bear
that name, he contended, belong to all the
Catholics, who constitute their sovereign people, and this people wills the supremacy of
the Pope and has the right to impose it.

This service to the majority of the Catholics
put that party in a humor to ask other services,
and Thiers was found very willing to render
them. He had been greatly struck, at the time
of the February Revolution, with the attitude of
the clergy toward the Orleans Monarchy. Guizot had said from the Tribune, " The clergy was
not exiled with Charles X., but it was dethroned
with him." Even so moderate a revolution as
this could not, however, be well received by a
dominion-loving hierarchy. The clerical party
had been dissatisfied even with the Restoration
Government, which had in its service more of
the indifferent than of the faithful, and had been
treated by the Government of Louis Philippe
with respect rather than with favor. Accordingly, it is widely believed that from 1830
to 1848 the priests were persecuted. Readers
will recall the exclamation of the old monk
who, having lost in the cloister the notion of
time and of revolutions, was expelled from his
monastery in 1881 : " Will this Louis Philippe
never cease to persecute us? " Thiers was too

just to reproach the Guizot Government with
the measures which he himself had helped defend ; but he saw in the clerical party one of the
forces that perhaps contributed to the fall of
the Monarchy, and that had more than once
compelled it to yield. Having been formidable
adversaries, they would be useful auxiliaries.
He therefore received Falloux's propositions
kindly, almost eagerly. The only thing the
clergy and their friends could ask was precisely
what had been denied them under monarchical
governments, — the right of instruction, and a
definitive victory in their conflict of centuries
against the University.

The sentiments of the University were pretty
much the same as those which had actuated the
authors of the July Revolution. It was but a
few years since the most eminent statesmen of
the time had defended the University in the
Chamber of Peers against Montalembert. Out
of this discussion grew the Bill of 1844, upon
which Thiers had made a very favorable report to the lower House. What was asked of
him was therefore really a concession ; still, he
had never exhibited much zeal for the diffu-
sion of education, and was inclined to regard
it as an impracticable dream of the doctrinaires,
especially of Guizot. Thiers reproached the
professors with having too readily received the

new ideas; he found fault with the extension
given to scientific studies; he even complained
that too much time was given to Greek, — not
because, as Cousin with friendly insolence
taunted him, he did not know Greek, but because he preferred the stern and practical
genius of ancient Rome. And indeed if the
professors were a little inclined toward the
Left, the mass of the teachers had passed to
the extreme Left, and threatened to wield a
dangerous influence upon the elections.

All this made less unpleasant the concession which he was asked to make to the public
interest. Nevertheless, his support of the
Law of 1850 has been characterized as a re-
cantation and as a conversion, — two words of
sinister sound to the ears of a public man. In
an able speech he exonerated himself from the
charge of instability by the only method that
satisfies a serious man at such a time, — not
by denying any change, but by explaining it
on the ground of changed circumstances. In
reading this speech, one perceives that he had
made every effort to save all that could be
saved of the interests of knowledge and reason.
But he could not completely defend the radical
defect of a law which delivered our youth and
our society over to the contention of two opposite forces, from whose collision a shock

was as certain as from the collision of two clouds oppositely charged with electricity. If parties have since that day hardened into sects, the embodiment of the Falloux principles in the Law of 1850 has had its share in the result. It is scarcely necessary to add that nobody was satisfied, perhaps not even the authors of the Bill. Guizot attacked it in the " Journal des Débats," M. Jules Simon in his " Freedom of Thought," M. Barthélemy Saint-Hilaire from the Tribune, in the name of the University. On the other hand, the Ultramontane press and the hierarchy showered their anathemas upon M. de Falloux. It was a genuine compromise.

This and other sacrifices to the spirit of the time have often been regretted. What a time, and what a spirit! The President of the Republic made it his business to bring to nought the most intelligent efforts, and would have broken up the most united of parties. In order to foil him it would have been necessary to foresee his course. His policy consisted in promising the democratic party a government more in harmony with their wishes than that of the Assembly, and in promising the middle class a repose untroubled by agitations, interpellations. and ministerial crises. To this some Royalists added, of their own accord, the hope that the Prince would yield the supreme power to their king. The policy was much the same as that of the first Bonaparte, minus the greatness.

The conflict between the two powers arose in the simplest way in the world. The commander of the army at Paris was General Changarnier, who, although but slightly devoted to the Republic, was looked to as the defender of law, and consequently of the Assembly. This position, together with his worth and real dignity of character, made him a considerable personage. His relation to the President recalled that of the Duke of Guise to Henry III. The General also said, " He would not dare!" when a possible dismissal was spoken of. The future Napoleon III. did, however, dare to dismiss him abruptly, and the Assembly felt keenly the insult and the danger. It was on the occasion of the interpellation provoked by this first act of the conspiracy that Thiers delivered one of his ablest speeches. He resumed the place which he had abandoned in favor of a public interest whose pressing importance he had exaggerated, and became once more the undisputed leader of the Liberal party, — a place which he thenceforward retained to the last.

His speech was a model of the prophetic

good-sense in which he was unequalled. He made a detailed history of the aid and support given by the Chamber to the President, whom he reproached with offensive ingratitude, and closed with the following memorable words : —

" Permit me this remark : when one of two powers in the State has encroached on the other, it is indeed annoying to the encroaching power to yield ; but if it be the invaded power that yields, its weakness is made so patent to all eyes that it is lost. I add but one word : there are to-day in our Government but two powers, the executive power and the legislative power. If the Assembly yields to-day, there will remain but one. And from the moment when there shall be but one power in the State, the form of the government will be changed. The name, the title, may come when it will ; that matters little to me. But the thing that you say you do not wish, you will obtain this very day if you yield. There remains, then, but one power, I repeat ; the name will come in time. The Empire is established ! "

This was not Thiers' last speech in that Assembly, but these were his last political counsels. They display a sentiment compatible even with the Republic of 1848, but incompatible with anything looking toward a dictatorship. They are the expression of a slowly formed, definitive opinion to which he remained faithful. He took no part in discussing the proposed revision of the Constitution, — a plan devised by shrewd fomenters of disorder, who saw that it would be easier to suppress the Republic by process of law than to overthrow it by force. An article in the Constitution made a two-thirds majority necessary for revision; and as more than a third of the Assembly was composed of Republicans who would not take part in the perilous game, the measure could not be carried. But the proposition was a blow to the Constitution; it excused — almost exonerated beforehand — those who should violate the Constitution; it called in question the organization, and therefore the very existence, of the Republic. The measure failed by nearly a hundred votes, but the legal basis of the Republic was shaken.

This legal basis was once more supported by Thiers in the sitting of Nov. 17, 1851. The discussion turned upon the then famous proposition of the Questors, who claimed for the Assembly the right of calling out the army in order that the legislative body should not be at the mercy of its enemies. No sober man would deem hesitation possible touching this legitimate and modest proposal; nevertheless, it was rejected. The Assembly was so bitterly divided, that each faction suspected its neighbor of an intention to make illegal use of this legal force, and so a strange coalition was organized against the only means of safety. These are the evil days of parliaments, when they make good all the slanders of their enemies; when rage, rancor, rivalry, cloud all notions of justice and of foresight. But these occasional faults of parliaments are permanent in absolute governments. This was shown a few weeks later. The *coup d'état* was accomplished, and free discussion, — the pledge of all security and of all freedom, — political morality, real order (for order is not another name for silence), solid and lasting peace, everything that makes for the honor of a nation, disappeared in a night.

CHAPTER IV.

THE EMPIRE (1851–1863).

THIERS felt the woes of France as other men feel the heart-breaking sorrows of private life. He has been known to shed tears in the Tribune over the distresses of his conquered country. By the side of his grief at the defeat of freedom, exile and imprisonment were trifles. This unexpected proscription could not in the least further the plans of the author of the *coup d'état*. Of what avail was mere eloquence against material force? The Assembly once dissolved, Thiers was but a helpless, inoffensive citizen. He received, however, precisely the same treatment as the heads of the army. Early in the morning of the 2d of December, 1851, he was taken from his house in St. George Place, and sent under escort, first to the prison of Mazas, then to that of Ham, finally to Brussels, where he received notification of his exile. Messrs. de Lasteyrie, de Rémusat, Duvergier de Hauranne, Baze, Roger, after a week at Mazas, were by the same decree exiled from France. The exile of the Princes of Orleans was at the same time confirmed, and aggravated by the confiscation of their estates. This, according to M. Dupin, who soon became Attorney-General at the Court of Appeals, was "the first flight of the eagle."

The exiles passed the first months — sometimes together, sometimes dispersed — at Brussels, at London, in Switzerland. In July, as Thiers was preparing to set out for Italy, he suddenly learned from the "Moniteur Officiel" of a decree authorizing the victims of the former arbitrary decree to return to their homes. The same whim that had shut the doors of France opened them again, and no attempt at an explanation broke the universal silence. This was the beginning of that illogical series of shocks which characterized the policy of the next eighteen years. With more or less eagerness every one took advantage of this permission, with all the gratitude which we owe, said Thiers, "to the man who returns a watch that he has stolen."

"Augustus re-established order, which is only another name for lasting servitude; for when a usurper has seized the sovereignty of a free State, the name of law is given to whatever tends to confirm the unbounded authority of a single man, and the name of disturbance, dissension, misgovernment, to whatever tends to maintain the honorable freedom of subjects." These words of Montesquieu describe in a masterly way the spectacle awaiting the exiles at their return; for if the manifestations of freedom are always new, the proceedings of despotism are extremely monotonous. Rarely, however, has a country so quickly and completely forgotten all the principles for which it had fought and suffered. Like Balzac's Rastignacs and Marsays, the masters of France had seen a speculation upon Change as well as a *coup d'état* in the complot whereby they had risen to power; and Thiers must have felt as Lafayette did on his return from captivity at Olmütz, — that France had become dwarfed since his departure.

If by the aid of some historical reminiscences and of some contempt for human kind, it was possible to explain the profound calm which had succeeded the agitations of a free country, the boldest invention would have been taxed to imagine how quickly this calm was to be disturbed by the very man whose interests it seemed to subserve. The assumption appeared reasonable that President Louis Bonaparte, who had made himself Emperor under the singularly chosen name of Napoleon III.,

would give absolute repose to a country which
no longer found scope either for its imagination
or for its vanity in the cultivation of politics.
This seemed the more probable, inasmuch as the
master himself had little taste for affairs, and a
real passion for pleasure. But observers reckoned without that peculiar trait of the Bona-
partes, — the desire to make themselves felt
in the affairs of the world; a desire which,
after all, makes them great, and separates them
from vulgar adventurers. The nation wished to
sleep; it was promptly awakened. Men were
looking forward to a peaceful and sluggish life
under a moderate despotism, when suddenly,
after having formed an Imperial Court, which
was displeasing enough to an equality-loving
people, the Emperor contracted a marriage of
love, which cut him off from all the rest of the
crowned heads. Having promised peace, he
set about making war everywhere, and on all
pretexts, — in the Crimea, in Syria, in China,
in Mexico, in Italy; he even threatened England with invasion. And every day brought
some unexpected official address, some edict of
the Senate, some amendment to the Constitution, some imperial journey abroad or to
Algiers, some revolution in the palace, or,
what was much the same thing, some change
of ministry.

Worse yet, even the boasted safeguard against social disturbances seemed at times ready to disappear. The report was suddenly circulated that the Emperor was a socialist. Banks, treasuries, economic novelties of all kinds, were proposed by him, and made the subjects of protracted discussions by the great deliberative bodies of the State. These projects would disturb the public for a while, only to be pigeon-holed by functionaries more addicted to routine, perhaps wiser, than their masters. And the good people who, thinking themselves well rid of troublesome discussions, had rejoiced at the dissolution of the Assembly, were obliged to hear from a loftier tribune phrases announcing the most frightful intentions. For example, when the Emperor's aid was called for against the seditious demagogues of the great cities, he said to them, " My fibre answers to yours,"—a phrase as distasteful to linguistic as to political conservatives.

Thiers used to relate that one day the Duke of Wellington, wearied at the Council-board by the lengthy harangues of Lord Harrowby, exclaimed, " My Lord, you have too much education for your intelligence ! " It may be said that the Emperor had too much imagination, not for his intelligence, but for his power of concentration, — too many ideas for his executive faculty. As Thiers said, he frequently confused the verb *dream* (*rêver*) with the verb *reflect*. Now France has the habit of mistaking both the proposals of its deputies and the lucubrations of its sovereigns for dangerous realities; and thus real difficulties are increased by imaginary apprehensions. Here, all was not a dream; this mental activity of Napoleon III., by arousing curiosity, criticism, attention, disturbed the slumber that every despot must be anxious to produce; and when, finally, he was compelled to grant some shadow of freedom, he had to encounter all the hatred of the first day, embittered by all the errors of more than a decade.

During the first epoch of the Empire, Thiers took no part in politics. He limited himself to some bit of advice, rarely followed, touching foreign affairs, or to some warning to one of the diplomatists who frequented Parisian society as well as the ministerial bureaux. This society was at that time very brilliant. That portion, especially, which rather insolently styles itself the *grand monde* was then, despite the misfortunes of the time, thoroughly amusing. Talleyrand used to say that one who had not seen the *salons* of 1789 could not know the pleasure of living. This judgment was doubtless partly due to the fact that Talleyrand was

9

then young, but also quite as much to the circumstance that good society was then unanimous in its taste for free government and
enlightened philosophy. Likewise in 1852,
Parisian society was very hostile to the revived
Empire. Everybody agreed in cursing despotism, and academicians who had seen so many of
their fellows arrested; partisans of the royal families whose princes were proscribed and ruined;
parliamentarians in mourning for freedom of
speech; men of the middle class irritated by
the pretensions of the Court; aristocrats who
ridiculed that vulgar Court with its petty magnificence; members of the liberal professions
who felt oppressed or threatened, — all united
to exchange those sarcasms, those anecdotes,
which are the delight of the *salon*. At no
time, perhaps, has French society been more
divorced from the government, and one might
frequent it for a long time without meeting a
partisan of the established régime. If, as he
alleged, the Emperor had saved society, the
claim was not acknowledged by *good* society.
Here all were irreconcilable: Legitimists, Republicans, Orleanists, Liberals, gave one another
the hand. It was then that "the Liberal
Union" was formed. This was neither a secret
society nor an organization; the members were
bound by no positive engagement, but by the

simple understanding that when the mistakes of the Empire should cause its inevitable downfall, its enemies should all stand shoulder to shoulder, whatever the free government that might succeed, whether republic or monarchy. It is possible to see some trace of this disposition in the first deliberations of the National Assembly of 1871.

M. Thiers took a brilliant part in the racy conversations of the élite of Paris, and it was at this time that he most freely gratified his social tastes. As a natural result of his mode of life, his conversation had become refined, his habits had grown more delicate and more elegant, while at the same time society had accustomed itself to whatever was peculiar or original in his manners. Two things are requisite to success in the *salon:* one must be like others, and yet one must have some note of distinction from others. From the social standpoint, it is as fatal to be like everybody as to be like nobody; and superior men, along with the rest, are subject to this law. It is needless to say that in Thiers the element of originality was very marked. Nevertheless, he was thoroughly amiable in his relations with men, and he exhibited a delicate gallantry toward women. To this gallantry it cannot be said that all were entirely insensible.

Thiers carried into society — no easy thing — a jealous patriotism. Before the interests of France all party zeal died out in him, and he never in the slightest degree shared the feeling of an *émigré.* During the Crimean War no one wished more heartily for the success of our arms; and the Emperor felt this so strongly that he referred to Thiers in a public discourse as "the illustrious national historian." It was not merely as a patriot, however, that Thiers took an interest in the war; he saw his plans of 1840 being realized by that same army of the July Government whose most distinguished captains were now in exile. He occupied himself very much with the matter, and his opinions sometimes reached the imperial ear. M. Mérimée, who had been drawn to the Empire by his opinions, and still more by his affections, was one of the few who saw both parties. This Saint-Evremond of our century deserved this exceptional position by his freedom of mind and his trustworthiness. One evening in 1855, when Mérimée chanced to be present in the *salon* of St. George Place, Thiers warmly pointed out certain measures that should be taken and certain things that should be said, in the critical situation in which France then stood. Mérimée, thinking to be useful to both, repeated the conversation to the

Emperor. "You will thank M. Thiers," returned the Emperor, "but he is not at the centre of the situation. He is accustomed to address a Chamber actuated by patriotic sentiments and opinions; we live in different times!"

The epigrams of the *salons* and a few bits of political advice were mere trifles in the mental activity of a man who had erewhile filled Europe with his policy and with his deeds. Before speaking of the great work upon which he was engaged, it must be added that he acquired at this time a taste for the sciences. He had learned little of them in his youth, the colleges of the First Empire having been weak on this side. At times, however, his alert curiosity had turned him in that direction; even under the Restoration he had taken lessons in algebra. He now turned his attention chiefly to the natural sciences and to astronomy. Sometimes he spent the whole night star-gazing at the Observatory, and he followed the researches of Pasteur at the Normal School. He even caused Plateau's fine experiment on the formation of the world to be repeated. His mind certainly gained in severity by these attempts, and some trace of this discipline is to be found in his speeches. But science cannot be cultivated without those preliminary studies for which he had neither taste nor time; and to the fruitful invention of scientific ideas, a thorough acquaintance with what others have thought is indispensable. Now, Thiers cared little to know what others had thought; intellectually, others scarcely existed for him. It was therefore not very safe for him to venture upon this new ground. In the natural and physical sciences, more than elsewhere, it is necessary to be on one's guard against the desire for clearness. That which seems extremely clear and neat is very apt not to be true. Although Voltaire's science is not to be despised, one feels that he prefers the risk of seeming superficial to that of not being understood; and Thiers is open to much the same reproach. He wrote, however, a book upon these subjects, demonstrating to his own satisfaction the theory of necessary ideas in scientific philosophy; and one of his speeches, a few years later, set forth the analogous theory of necessary liberties. This work is not sufficiently finished to be published and exposed to the criticism of professional scholars, who have but little indulgence for amateurs. Chamfort has an anecdote of a Genevan law professor, who concluded a rapturous eulogy of Voltaire's universality with the remark, " It is only in public law that I find him a bit deficient." " And for my part," said Dalemberg, "it is only in geometry that I find him a bit deficient."

Thiers' best diversion during these years was the completion of his "History of the Consulate and the Empire."[1] Sainte-Beuve had spoken of the first volumes with an admiration that was more than justified by the later ones, — the chances and changes of the author's life having brought him the deeper knowledge of men and affairs for which we pay so dear. It has been asserted that he inferred too much from his own experience; that the *coup d'état* of December 2 (1851) led him to scan with greater suspicion that of the 18th Brumaire; that Napoleon III. opened his eyes concerning Napoleon I.; and that he thenceforward judged the First Empire in the light of the Second. If experience — which in spite of popular prepossessions is so rarely instructive — had led him to think of these two sovereigns what Tacitus said of Augustus, *Cuncta fessa recepit,* — "The Commonwealth being exhausted, he took command of it," — there would have been no great harm. But the truth is, that if there be

---

[1] The first five volumes appeared in 1845; the sixth and seventh, in 1847; the eighth and ninth, in 1849; the tenth, eleventh, and twelfth, in 1851; the thirteenth and fourteenth, in 1856; the fifteenth and sixteenth, in 1857; the seventeenth and eighteenth, in 1860; and the last two, in 1861 and 1862.

any difference in Thiers' judgments before and after 1851, the Emperor himself is to blame, rather than his nephew. Can it be maintained that Napoleon is the same man from the first days of the Consulate to the last days of the Empire? How could the author treat in the same manner the great captain who gave lustre to the French name, and the indefatigable gambler who constantly set our destinies at stake on the bloody gaming-table of the battlefield? General Bonaparte, as Chief Magistrate, was irreproachable; such was the opinion of his country and of impartial Europe. He was not only a moderate restorer, — he was able and fertile, original and brilliant. He made France live in an atmosphere of security, of hope, and of admiration. The origin of his power, the forms of his government, the means by which he sustained it, certainly do not commend themselves to liberal opinion. But historians are not doctors of constitutional law. The historian must take men as they are, and judge them according to their times. The Government of the First Consul was incomparably humaner, juster, more regular, than either the Old Régime or the Convention, — the sources whence came all the barbarism that still clung to it.

The opposite reproach — that of loving his

hero too much — has been more frequently raised, and seems better justified. A volume could indeed be made up of passages containing condemnations, in sharp, stern terms, of the Emperor's faults. But it is true that Thiers passionately admires his hero; that he loves even when he chastens. He keeps back none of the faults, but these faults sadden him, and he suggests all that can be said in extenuation of genius gone astray.

Even those who have never been carried away by this passion cannot deny that it is a powerful source of interest. The current of feeling that bears the reader through the windings of this immense work is strengthened by the seduction of which the author is himself a victim, and it is hard to wish him less prepossessed. Nevertheless, this disposition tends to give Napoleon, as he appears in this book, a somewhat conventional character. The Emperor is a despot, but the author will have it that he is the ideal despot. Napoleon had too much wit not to know how to charm and win over, when it suited his ends to do so; but it does not follow that this morose and haughty, distrustful and irritable person, was the most amiable of men. His practical and statesman-like spirit made him averse to needless cruelty when his power was not at stake; at times he exhibited some emotion upon counting the slain. But is it possible to admit that humanity and pity were habitual to this great consumer of human life? Thiers inclines to attribute to Napoleon the gentler qualities of his own heart. The historian sees works of genius in the battles he describes so well, but he could not have witnessed these battles without being stirred to compassion. So, in his narrative, war resembles a chess-game, and in order to defend his hero he endeavors to separate him into two different beings. " In war, the Emperor was prompted by his genius; in politics, by his passions." A great poet has likewise said, " It was not Rolla who controlled his life, it was his passions! " [1] But do not the passions and the genius of a man make up the man himself? The responsibility lies neither with his passions nor with his genius, but with the whole being called Napoleon.

An incomplete analysis of the Emperor's character; an almost complete forgetfulness of what was going on abroad, especially in England; blindness to the quite genuine movement of independence and hostility, even in the very circle of the sovereign after 1812; too much indulgence for the unjustifiable return from

[1] Alfred de Musset, " Rolla," ii.

Elba, — these are the faults which are atoned for by such great qualities. To the last page the author shows unabated zeal and attention to detail. Twenty years of his life were devoted to this work. For a professional historian the time would not be excessive, and the task becomes prodigious when one reflects that during one half this time the author was a busy public man overtaken by two revolutions, and during the other half a man of the world beguiled by a thousand artistic and scientific fancies. Yet this history is distinguished from the great models by its more faithful and more intelligible account of the way in which public business is transacted. It pictures political action. This colder side of history is never tiresome, — what we understand well is seldom so. In this, Thiers was an innovator, for he alone was capable of giving life to the bureaucratic side of human affairs. He treats everything with winning and communicative vivacity, and even when his thought is not very new, all that he thinks strikes him so keenly as to give the reader a sense of great freshness and novelty. What others appropriate he seems to discover; so that if he remarked, for example, that fortune is inconstant, you would think that you heard it for the first time. It is from himself that all the value and effect

of what he says proceeds; this personal element gives life to masses of the dullest details,
and renders readable a style which is too often
lacking in relief and distinction. In the pref-
ace to his twelfth volume he himself sets forth
the conditions of the historic style, — conditions which he reduces to the single requisite of
transparency. Style should resemble the best
plate-glass; whatever renders it perceptible is
a flaw.

In laying down the laws of the historic style,
Thiers naturally described his own, just as
Boileau in his " Poetic Art " set forth the rules
of his own composition. This does not necessarily imply that there is but one way of writing history, — that it is not permitted to display the talents of a romancer like Augustin
Thierry, of a poet like Lamartine, of a physi-
ologist like Michelet. But the truth is that the
political history of our century is best written with simplicity, with detail, with lucidity,
and that it cannot be otherwise conceived
without violating the condition of scrupulous
exactitude. Did Thiers conform to this indispensable condition? In this respect, critics
have done him the most uniform justice. They
have noted divergencies of opinion rather
than deviations from fact, and confirmation
has often come from the most unexpected

quarters. Thus Prince Metternich wrote to
Lady Westmoreland: [1]—

"I had never expected to find in a French book
a veracious account of the course of Austrian policy
in the years 1812 and 1813, — least of all from the
pen of M. Thiers, whom I have never met except
briefly on two occasions, and whose decided adversary I have been throughout his different ministries.
Latterly I have often been asked by men of importance, 'Are you not writing?' My uniform reply
has been, 'All that I could write is laid away in the
archives for the use of the historians of the future.' To-day I can refer those who may be curious
to inform themselves, to the fifteenth volume of
M. Thiers' History."

[1] April 4, 1857. Memoirs, viii. 417.

CHAPTER V.

THE EMPIRE (1863-1870).

WHILE these years of free labor and well-employed leisure were passing so pleasantly for Thiers, and while France was losing sight of the orator in the writer, a great change announced itself. The Emperor, perhaps wearied with warlike expeditions, perhaps yielding to some secret instinct which told him that the French were again possessed by the passion for change, took it into his head to propose and consequently to carry out (for he was the sole master) certain modifications in the Constitution of 1852. This Constitution was simply organized despotism: no freedom of the press, no electoral liberty, no parliamentary freedom. The Emperor alone addressed the Chambers, which had not even the right to present an address in reply. The Budget and the laws were voted by the deputies, it is true, but they had the right neither to modify the Budget nor to amend the laws. Worse still, the reports of the sessions were not published. There appeared only an abbreviated analysis of the proceedings in the Official Journal, written in the third person by the editor, who was a mere clerk. When some one happened to speak to the Emperor of the orators of the Corps Législatif, he remarked ironically, "Why, I know of but one, — M. Denis Lagarde."[1] The ministers did not sit in the Assembly, and had neither responsibility nor solidarity.

To educe from these elements a liberal Constitution would have been difficult, nor did the Emperor think of it. He did not make the electors free, he hardly modified the press-laws, he permitted the ministers to be dependent upon no power save his favor; but he permitted the deputies to speak and even to reply to him with a respectful address. He appointed a special minister, without a cabinet and without responsible authority, whose function was to defend the active ministers without taking any part in their proceedings. So a lawyer who pleads for a criminal before the police court is cognizant of the facts only after the offence. This was a first step in the direction of parliamentary government, toward which all civilization

[1] The clerk-editor in question. — TR.

tends or to which it returns. The objections to the system are obvious: an opposition Chamber would easily have unmasked the real author behind his attorney, just as the police justice punishes the accused; and the attorney would not have been long supported by a ministry whose plans had been shipwrecked in the Assembly. But the conception, strange as it was, constituted a step forward, and the public interest required that Liberal leaders should not be too exacting. The opportunity was a tempting one to speak to France of her rights and interests, without too narrowly scrutinizing the rectitude of the mind that had conceived these reforms. Accordingly, upon the announcement of the general elections of 1863 (the first since the Reform), there was a conference, at the house of the late Duke of Broglie, of the leaders of the several parliamentary parties. They discussed the opportunity of entering the Corps Législatif, and of trying their chances before the few constituencies where success was possible.

The step was a serious one. There was in the Chamber an opposition group made up of distinguished orators, who were styled the Five: Messrs. Picard, Jules Favre, Emile Ollivier, Darimon, and Hénon; they were for the most part young men who had given hostages to none of the old parties, and who had been neither exiled nor arrested by the Empire. Thus they could take oath without scruple, and could discuss every question upon its merits. The representatives of the old parties, as they were called, General Cavaignac and M. Carnot, had hitherto sought in the elections only an opportunity for protesting and for refusing the oath. The Broglie Conference had therefore to decide upon an important change of front on the part of the public men present. If they became deputies, they would be obliged to relinquish the attitude of absolute, uncompromising opponents of the Empire. Apart from the not very agreeable formality of the oath, honor commands those who by entering the Assembly assume a share in the government, not only to abstain from conspiring against that government, but not to attempt in any wise to overturn it, to regard themselves as no longer strangers to power, — in a word, to limit themselves to a constitutional opposition. Their conscience binds them to vote only for laws which they would propose were they members of the Ministry. If their opinions prevail in the Chamber, they may not refuse, if called upon, to attempt to carry them out in action.

In the Broglie Conference some declared this effort to be beyond the strength of their impartiality. They could be nothing but eternal enemies of the Empire, and could be satisfied by nothing short of its fall. The majority thought, however, that the useful task of spreading the truth, of discussing the Budget and the laws, and, by means of Constitutional Amendments of which the Emperor had first set the example, of attaining the government of the people by the people, was sufficient to justify the sacrifice of some grudges and of some hopes. After a serious discussion the acceptance of candidatures was agreed upon.

Thiers was not present at the Conference. He approved its resolutions, but was at first averse to the thought of himself carrying them out, and thus sacrificing his leisure, his tastes, his freedom of speech, perhaps his friendships. He was now sixty-six years old; would he feel at home in the Tribune, the steps of which he had not mounted since he was fifty-four? He decided, however, to set the example, and accepted two candidacies, one at Valenciennes and one at Paris. He was elected only at Paris, for electoral liberty did not exist in the provinces, and scarcely any of his friends were elected with him. Paris has never better justified her claim to be a refuge for the Oppo-

sition, and M. de Persigny's violent proceedings tended to make the election a personal
defeat for the Emperor. This placed Thiers
in a false light, for he was always respectful
even to mere *de facto* governments.

It was a great day for France and for the
intellectual world, and many young hearts beat
faster, when Thiers rose for the first time in the
Imperial Parliament. He did not ascend the
Tribune, which was reserved for the Imperial
Advocate. He spoke from his place in the
House, and all eyes were fastened upon that
well-known face. His eyes gleamed with
shrewdness, and appeared, as he looked over
his spectacles, to strike to the very souls of
his hearers. They remarked his attitude, familiar but serious, and his white hair which
bore witness to a long and glorious past.
With what feelings they heard his voice and
caught that Provençal accent which lends pi-
quancy to the commonest words! Everything
about him suggested that he had been con-
jured up from another age to redeem us from
the sombre future we already foreboded.
France, silent for a dozen years, had found a
voice again in the most French of her children,
and the fire and force of her spokesman were
unabated by age. With his accustomed art
he adapted himself to a new situation, to a

suspicious power which must not be irritated, to unknown and distrustful auditors quick to take alarm, to an outside public difficult to please in the matter of opposition.

This political manifesto (Jan. 14, 1864) begins with an account of our revolutions and of the mistakes of the past, and ends with an enumeration of the conditions indispensable to any government. These conditions are simply and happily described as "the essential liberties," — freedom of the press, electoral liberty, parliamentary freedom, and ministerial responsibility. The Empire was very far from realizing these liberties; yet there is nothing revolutionary in the demand for them. An enlightened conservative might subscribe to it. To prove, however, that his intention was not to destroy but to build up, he described his own attitude toward what were then called "the old parties," and toward the past which he was accused of wishing to revive. Shall we not find here a good lesson in personal dignity and in political morality?

"The French soil is covered with the wrecks of these governments. There live men who are termed the representatives of the old parties. I am one of these representatives ; and I ask you, in the name of our common country, for permission to put aside every veil. I have observed our country, and I think

I know her well. What mission has she intrusted to these representatives of the old parties? She has given them the mission of studying public affairs, of discussing these affairs with sincerity and impartiality, but also of probing them. She has given them the mission of watching over the public good, of watching over the progressive and continuous development of our institutions ; for the good administration of public affairs is bound up in good institutions. Such is the mission which she has given to the representatives of the old parties. Should these representatives, instead of devoting themselves to this task, show any intention to substitute one form of government for another, one dynasty for another, they would instantly become weak ; for they would be going beyond their authority.

" As concerns myself, I have served an august family, to-day unfortunate. I owe it the respect which we cannot refuse to great sorrows nobly borne. I owe it the affection we cannot but feel for those with whom we have passed the best portion of our lives. There is something which I do not owe, and which it does not ask, but which the pride of my soul willingly gives, — this is to live in retirement, and not let my old masters see me aspiring to the splendor of authority while they pine in exile. But there is one thing which — I call Heaven to witness ! — they do not ask of me, which they will never ask, and I shall never give, and that is, to sacrifice to them the interests of my country. I therefore here declare as an honest man, that if this essential freedom is granted us, for my part I shall accept it, and shall take my place among the submissive and grateful citizens of the Empire. But if it be our duty to accept, permit me to say to you that it is the duty of the Government to give. Let it not be supposed that I speak the language of arrogant exaction! No; I know that in order to obtain, one must ask with respect. It is therefore with respect that I ask it. But gentlemen must beware! Our fiery country, to-day half asleep, whose exaggerated desires are so prone to flame up, — this country which permits me to-day to ask in her behalf in the most deferential tone, will perchance one day require."

The last words were bold, and he alone could pronounce them; but the dexterity of the entire discourse will be noted, and its gradations in substance and in form. By dint of thus skilfully weighing his words, Thiers was enabled, throughout the remainder of the Empire, to ally a very keen opposition with opinions as moderate and as statesmanlike as ever. Inflexible as to the essential conditions of parliamentary government, hostile to personal power, he is often found in agreement with the sentiments — especially the concealed ones — of members of the majority, touching our foreign policy, Italy, the temporal power, the protectionist system. It cost him neither effort nor sacrifice to be agreeable to the timid or the prudent, while the frankness and vivacity of his assertions of right gave genuine strength to liberal France; and the authority of his name, the solidity and clearness of his arguments, forced the Government to reply more seriously and more definitely. The public which he addressed had been stirred to a certain vague anxiety by the renewed caprices of an autocratic master. Having indulged the thought that this master would make no mistakes, the public had been willing not to see the mistakes which he really made. But the time was coming when no one was sorry to see these mistakes pointed out and prevented, even at the risk of the modest liberties the value of which was beginning to be felt.

Thiers' very compromising attitude sometimes ruffled his friends of the Left, — for he was happily not alone in the Corps Législatif. There was M. Ernest Picard, that bright and sensible speaker; M. Jules Favre, a satirical, impassioned, correct improviser; M. Emile Ollivier, whose southern eloquence gradually became colored with the neutral tints of a liberal Empire; M. Berryer, whose thrilling voice had not lost its deep accents; M. Jules Simon, as witty and as dramatic as any, eager to defend not only political truths, but those of morals and humanity. They could not all follow Thiers in his forbearance toward the Government, and declared themselves more irreconcilable than he. They trusted to the natural mobility of our nation, which is rather prompt to overturn than able to reform, and to the inconsistency of imperial institutions with freedom.

For seven years Thiers gave his countrymen lessons in home and foreign politics in these speeches permeated with lucid good-sense. His limpid exposition would alone have made him practically influential as an orator. Never has a speaker succeeded better in accentuating positive reason, in giving point to commonplace. His anxiety to instruct is too obvious, and he is sometimes prolix; but his prolixities are delightful episodes, or ingenious historical parallels of which no hearer could ever have been weary.

Though rhetorical precepts and examples have never been of much use to any one, it is interesting to know Thiers' method of preparing a speech. After having laid out the general plan, he devoted his hours to the most assiduous researches, sparing neither time nor trouble, questioning specialists persistently and hearing them patiently, collecting a mass of materials sufficient for the composition of a book. Next he considered

and winnowed his notes, distributing them to
the various divisions of his subject. He wrote
out, not the speech, but the order of his ideas;
and then began the strangest preparation. In
the evening, when his friends were gathered
in his drawing-room, he turned the conversation to the subject with which he was occupied. This was an easy matter, for wherever
he talked, the conversation was not apt to be
discursive. Without throwing off the familiar
tone, he tried a fragment of his proposed
speech upon his companions, and gauged its
interest by their attention and their remarks.
It was in this first improvisation that parallels
and episodes occurred to him. It will be seen
that the method is an easy one.

It is very difficult to give an account of his
speeches; the true and interesting way to
judge them is to read them. One can do this
without fatigue in M. Calmon's excellent edition, with its clear and impartial " arguments,"
the ability of which justifies the important
part played by the editor in our Assemblies
during the last twenty years. As we must
choose some passages, let us leave one side
the developments of the essential liberties
(commonplaces to-day), the Roman Question,
the discussions of the Budget and of the
merchant marine service; let us even pass

over many charming pages like the following definition of a free country: —

"While discussing the true principles of political science, Machiavelli raises the question whether nations or princes are the more liable to err, and he reaches a conclusion which can be reduced to these words: Yes, a nation is liable to err, but less so than a man. And for the following reason. The individual makes mistakes. Why? Because, being master of his own actions, not being compelled to deliberate, to examine the pros and the cons, he allows himself to be swayed by his inclinations. Then he goes astray, and if he hold in his hands the fate of a nation, he may plunge it into grievous woes. But a free nation is a multiple and collective being; a free nation cannot form a decision without assembling, deliberating, weighing the pros and the cons; and thus it has that God-given security against error, — the obligation of consulting its reason. So having long reflected and often asked myself, in the course of a life already long, what is the true definition of a free nation, I have reached this one, which I leave to your meditations: a free nation is a being that thinks before it acts."

We must pass over all that is merely delightful or useful in these speeches, in order to recall that which is politic, prudent, almost prophetic. Thiers entered the Chamber in order to defend not only freedom but peace,

— peace which is always endangered by an imprudent policy. On this point he was an absolute conservative. In his speech of April 13, 1865, he said : —

" In speaking of domestic affairs, it is quite correct to say that there is a new policy. Kings have been compelled to share their authority with their people. Upper classes have been compelled to share their influence with middle or lower classes. And for all this new forms were indispensable. But in the matter of a foreign policy, whether I go back to the most political of ancient historians, Polybius, or to the most political of modern historians, Guicciardini, I find everywhere that foreign policy is simply the old-time prudence of a vigilant State, which never takes its eye off its neighbors, which hinders small States from growing great, great States from growing greater, or in any way becoming a source of apprehension; it is always, I say, the same old prudence and the same vigilance."

From this point of view Thiers must have been struck by what was taking place before his eyes. If the Holy Alliance of his youth, which had paralyzed our foreign policy, was somewhat weakened by the events of 1848, the Emperor's turbulent European policy tended to revive it under another form. At the very moment of the entrance of the new deputies to the Corps Législatif, the Mexican expedition, characterized by M. Rouher as "the finest thought of the reign," was being pushed forward for the sake of realizing a dangerous theory based upon ethnography, imagination, and operations at the Bourse. All this was far from reassuring to the positive spirit of Thiers, who was very severe toward the dreamy, romantic, and somewhat German side of Napoleon III. This remarkable personage has been described as a man of "unrecognized incapacity;" but he was unknown rather than unrecognized. Even his duplicity, the wonder and envy of the other sovereigns, was overdone. He got credit for his silence; it was believed that he was hatching some great design, when he was simply concealing himself. He was a sphinx who frequently had no enigma.

Reducing the Imperial foreign policy to its simplest terms, we can say that it was precisely the reverse of the opinions of Thiers, who would have permitted the formation of no great neighboring States. If, however, in spite of him, such States had been formed, he would have taken care to keep the peace with them until he had organized a strong army. Simple as this is, it is diametrically opposed to the policy of the Empire as expounded by M. Rouher. The upshot of that policy was to favor the creation of powerful

States, and then to pick dangerous quarrels
with them, while sacrificing the strength and
organization of the army for the sake of popularity. Thiers opposed the formation of the
kingdom of Italy, notwithstanding his admiration and friendship for Cavour, and the satisfaction of seeing a great liberal monarchy
beyond the Alps. He strongly advised intervention, in 1864, with reference to the question
of the duchies, of which Lord Palmerston said:
"But two persons thoroughly understood the
question of the duchies, — Prince Albert, who
is dead, and I, who have forgotten it." This is
a sufficient reason for not entering upon the
subject here.

Was it wise, in 1866, to allow Austria to be
conquered, and to rejoice over this sad presage
of our misfortunes? Here, again, Thiers felt a
disabling thrust at France, which would compel her, one day, to make a heroic effort to
repair the injury thus permitted. He foresaw
that dire extremity, the inevitable consequence
of so many mistakes, but he feared it too much
not to wish to postpone it. He therefore expressed himself so guardedly as not to irritate
the susceptibilities of France. To this double
aim his speech of March 14, 1867, was devoted.
The Liberals of that time have been accused
of counselling war, because they pointed out

the danger of the mistakes that had been made, and the way to lessen the consequences of these mistakes. The reader of this memorable speech sees how little justification there is for such a reproach, and how many catastrophes would have been averted had its clairvoyant counsels been followed. In this address, which is as literary as it is political, Thiers describes how he has been gradually liberalized by public events, and how his political education has been completed by a very near view of the workings of freedom and of absolutism, "the one redeeming France, the other compromising her!"

It is impossible to deny one's self the pleasure of transcribing a graceful passage from one of his speeches on Italy (April 13, 1865):

"For my part I have always regarded Italy as the Greece of the Middle Ages, and Florence as a true Christian Athens not inferior to the ancient city; and when one considers all that took place from the year 1000 to the year 1600, in that epoch so brilliant, so fruitful, so admirable, what is there in common, I ask you, between Venice, the mediæval queen of the sea, Venice more Asiatic than European, sharing none of the passions of Italy where she had scarce a foothold, and, after a long career of opulence, falling asleep in the arms of aristocracy and of pleasure, leaving us an imperishable memorial of her magnificence in the

thousand-tinted art of Titian and of Veronese, —
what is there in common between this aristocratic
Venice and democratic Florence : Florence, stretched
in the beautiful plains of the Arno, richer still by her
manufactures than was Venice by her ships ; Florence,
impelled by the pride of wealth to combat the feudal
aristocracy of the Ghibellines, and breathing into Italy
the Guelf passions with which she was fired ; Florence,
ending in the despotism of the Medici, those Cæsars
of peace, and destined to show forever the striking
features of the genius of civil war in her palaces,
which are merely embellished fortresses, in Dante's
deep and pathetic song inspired by the sorrows of
exile, in Machiavelli's solid knowledge wrung from the
experience of revolutions, in Michael Angelo's sternly
sublime art, so different from the coloring of Titian ? "

The times were becoming darker. There
had been reason to believe that the elections
of 1869 would result in an entirely new Corps
Législatif, which should prevent the final mistake, — "the only one that remained to be committed." Unhappily, the electoral oppression
was as stringent as ever, and the Emperor
could only " deceive himself again " by universal suffrage, as M. Ernest Picard put it. Few
opposition candidates succeeded in passing the
meshes of the official net. At Paris, Thiers
was elected only at a second ballot. But
Paris has seldom supported reform ; it drives

straight at revolution. In the provinces there was little numerical gain ; but Messrs. Gambetta, Jules Ferry, Grévy, Barthélemy Saint-Hilaire, Horace de Choiseul, were important accessions to the Liberal ranks. The movement of the popular mind was, however, so evident, the number of votes for opposition candidates so considerable, the discussion of the ratification of powers so unfavorable to the Administration, that the Emperor saw it was necessary to yield something. He accordingly prepared to grant a parliamentary Ministry. After much legislation he appointed M. Ollivier President of the Council and Minister of Justice, M. Buffet Minister of Finance, and M. Daru Minister of Foreign Affairs. This was indeed much. The late Duke of Broglie remarked, "We are at least out of the woods." The adhesion of others was less qualified. M. Masson became Prefect of the Department of the Nord, and M. Prévost-Paradol Minister to the United States. Both were to die upon seeing their hopes of freedom disappointed.

Never was a Reform Ministry better received. Thiers went so far as to say, in his speech of Jan. 27, 1870, "My opinions are to be found upon the Ministerial benches." Indeed, he and his friends were bound to rally to the support of any government that opened the

door to popular liberties. Those who still
harbored some distrust took care to dissemble
it. Everything indicates the Emperor's sincerity; but he was weak, and his deputies, his
high officials, his Court, his very household
continued to be borne along by the stream
upon which they had so long floated. How
could the limpid waters of freedom mingle with
this turbid stream without defilement? Of this
new freedom there was no guaranty, the Ministry not having the right to dissolve a hostile
Chamber where they were received with respectful antipathy. The Emperor, yielding to
his old habits of mind, — or rather to his former
friends and their perilous counsels, — could not
fail to revert to his fancy for a plebiscite. He
became infatuated with the plan of submitting
to universal suffrage, by *yes* or *no*, a Constitution in forty-five articles, without, of course,
permitting any choice among the articles.
M. Buffet's austere parliamentary spirit being
stirred at this, he promptly resigned, followed
closely by M. Daru.

How could M. Émile Ollivier fail to see, as
they saw, that this plebiscite impaired his authority, that the partisans of absolutism would be
emboldened by it, and that the politicians, who
were somewhat coldly yielding to the liberal
Empire, would be quite dissatisfied and discour-

aged? Full of confidence in the Emperor and in himself, he thought he could brave everything, and continue a parliamentary government between a small minority on the Left, and a majority on the Right which only sought an opportunity to regain the Imperial favor. In this session Thiers seldom spoke. His greatest speech is that of January 27, beginning upon the commercial treaties and ending upon general politics, under the influence of interrupters whose violence was a prelude to that of the latter days. He closed with these words: "I maintain that neither in public economy nor in politics do you exactly represent the country." This opinion was supported by only thirty-two votes against two hundred and twelve official deputies,— an excellent confirmation! For six months he relapsed into silence; but on the 30th of June he hotly demanded the contingent of ninety thousand men, which some of his opposition colleagues opposed, and which the Government abandoned. He would have preferred a levy of a hundred thousand men, as in the preceding years; and he pointed out that, without any thought of aggression, Government was bound to take into account the changes going on in Europe. By means of treaties of alliance, offensive and defensive, with the South German powers, Prussia—till recently a population of nineteen millions — now controlled upwards of forty millions. In this entirely pacific speech he said: —

"You will not see that Sadowa has doubled the Prussian power; you will not see that instead of a Germany all-powerful for defence, but powerless for aggression, — for the two principal monarchies, Prussia and Austria, could never agree upon a question of ambition, — you will not see that, instead of this inoffensive Germany, you have a formidable military Germany, which, to do it justice, does not seek to disturb the world, — for at its head is a superior man, a lover of peace, — but which makes it necessary for you to organize a more considerable military force, in order to be able to restrain any ambitious plans that might arise."

It is hardly possible to imagine words more moderate and more prudent. And what are we to think of a government which, the situation being understood, made bold to pick a quarrel with Germany, or, if you will, failed to prepare to defend itself in the event of a quarrel sought by the other side? In either aspect the blunder is equally culpable.

M. Daru was succeeded by the Duke of Gramont, who was thus unexpectedly placed in a Ministry whose opinions he did not at all share. Two days after Thiers' remarks, news was received that Marshal Prim had offered the crown of Spain to the Prince of Hohenzollern, a relative of the King of Prussia. The Minister was asked to inform the Chamber. Gramont confirmed the news, and, much more, declared that France would not permit a prince of his dynasty to ascend the throne of Charles V. He announced further that, the business being so serious, he would keep the Chamber informed from day to day. This was a declaration of war, or at least a piece of " hussar-diplomacy," to quote Doudan's expression. Thus Prussian self-respect was interested in an affair that would have been so easy to adjust quietly. Much worse ; as if it had been feared that Bismarck's prudent policy might foil these warlike plans, the king himself was directly addressed, so that a political question was more and more completely converted into a personal matter, — a dangerous course at any time.

In reply to the question addressed to him, the King of Prussia answered that he had seen no political bearing in the affair, and that it was as head of a family, and not as sovereign, that he had granted the permission to Prince Leopold. Almost at the same time it was learned that Spain did not insist, that the Prince renounced his claim, and that the King

of Prussia approved the renunciation. The
King even made an official statement of this
approbation. This was peace, and even a success for an imprudently conducted negotiation.

Strictly speaking, the Government might
have plumed itself upon this unlooked-for
success. But, by a fluctuation sufficiently explained by the intrigues of the Court and within the Ministry, and by the already morbid
indecision of the Emperor, the Government
bethought itself to demand of King William
a new concession. He was asked to pledge
himself, in the event of any change of mind on
the part of Spain or of the Prince, never in any
case to authorize the candidature of a Hohenzollern. This would have been a painful engagement for a haughty and powerful sovereign,
surrounded by a court of soldiers who desired
war. The King, vexed by these demands, —
which, to crown all, were addressed to him
personally, — replied that he could not pledge
himself forever, and that he reserved his freedom of action.

The French Ambassador, M. Benedetti, one
of the few able men of the Imperial diplomatic
service, thought this reply no more than what
was to be expected. The Minister, however,
required of him an additional step. Having
taken this step, the Ambassador was not of-

fended when the King replied through an aide-
de-camp that, having nothing new to communicate, he did not wish to resume the interview,
and that the business was concluded. This
was also the opinion of M. Benedetti, who
would not believe that these conversations
could result in war, without the interposition,
at a single point, of Bismarck and the Prussian
Ministry. It is only in tragedies that business
is transacted in this way between two sovereigns, or between a sovereign and an envoy.
Alas! on this occasion there ensued a tragedy
indeed, and a bloody one.

At this critical moment the Chamber was
asked, on the 15th of July, to vote a credit for
war expenses, and war was thus declared. It
was a triumph for the purely Bonapartist party,
which M. Émile Ollivier immediately joined,
either because he saw a real insult in the King's
attitude, or because he felt that he could not
desert the Emperor at such a conjuncture.
Perhaps he thought himself able to play the
dangerous game of snatching arms from his
adversaries' hands, and conceived the hope of
crowning the brow of the liberal Empire with
a halo of glory borrowed from the absolute
Empire.

Thiers could lend himself to none of these
schemes. He had long foreseen that the Em-

peror's blunders, the very existence of the Empire, the disproportionate growth of Prussia, the
inevitable rivalry of warlike nations, our humbled pride, all portended war; and he exerted
all his efforts to avert it, to delay it, to seek
alliances for France, to put her in the right in
the event of a conflict, and especially to organize an army worthy of France. This declaration of war, improvised upon a frivolous pretext
by an imprudent Minister, took Thiers by surprise. He knew that no preparations had been
made for this terrible conflict; that our army
was small, ill-drilled, and ill-equipped. He
saw his country thoughtlessly dragged into an
enterprise of which the authors suspected
neither the difficulties to be overcome nor the
dangers to be faced. And what a task to say
all this in public, without compromising France
and himself! It required a stoical devotion
to truth, to duty, to the Fatherland. He well
knew that his aims would be misinterpreted, his
person insulted. What hope could he cherish
of persuading a Chamber which was but too
happy to avenge itself in the name of a feigned
patriotism? What chance of averting the misfortune? He was certain to encounter not only
insincere outrages, but the frank indignation,
the insulting suspicions, of ignorant adversaries.
One must be a parliamentary veteran in order

to realize how difficult is the courage necessary to openly resist a Representative Assembly when it is fired, even without absolute sincerity, by a sentiment of national honor. In great public bodies there is a kind of physical action of man upon man that renders true for them the view which they vociferate. And it was Thiers, whose name had stood throughout half a century quite as much for the susceptibility of French honor as for political liberty, who, actuated by a patriotism too lofty to be understood, was to lead the forlorn hope.

The violence and vulgarity of the Chamber in that sitting of July 15, 1870, was unprecedented. The aim evidently was to prevent Thiers from speaking. This speech is therefore not to be cited as a model of oratorical art; it is merely the cry of the patriot and statesman. Through the storm of insult the following broken utterances were scarcely heard : —

" If there was ever a day, an hour, when it might be said without exaggeration that the Genius of History had her eyes fixed upon us, it is this day and this hour ; and surely such a reflection ought to make every one serious. . . . When war shall once be declared, no one will be more zealous, more eager than I to grant to Government all the means necessary to secure victory. . . . We cannot exaggerate the gravity

of the conjuncture. Remember that your decision
may result in the death of thousands of men. . . .
Remember the 6th of May, 1866 ! You then refused
to hear me when I pointed out to you the gathering
dangers. . . . Permit me to tell you that I regard
this war as egregiously imprudent. I love my country,
and no one was more painfully affected by the events
of 1866 ; but speaking from profound conviction, and
if I may venture to say so, from experience, I feel
that the occasion is ill-chosen. . . . If you do not
understand that at this moment I am performing the
most painful duty of my life, I pity you. . . . As to
myself, I am tranquil concerning the memory that
men will preserve of my action this day ; but I am
certain that you will see the day when you will regret
your haste. . . . Affront me, . . . insult me . . . !
I am ready to bear anything in order to spare the
blood of my fellow-citizens, which you are so imprudently ready to shed ! "

When the exhaustion consequent upon a
struggle of several hours compelled him to descend from the Tribune, the Minister replied
to him. A little refreshed by a moment's rest,
he resumed the unequal struggle against so
many men leagued together by the Fate pre-
siding over the falls of empires. What followed is well known. War was declared. The
Ollivier Ministry could not survive ; for not its
policy, but that begun on the 2d of December,

1851, was triumphant. After the violence of the Corps Législatif, Thiers was exposed to the insults of the street and of subservient newspapers. He suffered these things with proud-spirited contempt; and wrote, some days later, to a friend who had congratulated him upon his courage: —

Your letter touches me deeply. You have guessed all; the pretexts for the war are indeed pitiful.

It was certainly well to keep a vigilant eye upon Prussia, and to prepare to take revenge upon her; but mistakes are not so easily nor so promptly repaired. Especially on the present occasion was it important to wait, and we should infallibly have caught Prussia in straits. On that day we should have had on our side the whole of exasperated South Germany; Austria would have been compelled to declare herself; England would have been favorable instead of furious, and there would have been, withal, a means of restraining Russia. Until then our proper course was to live on from day to day, to settle all difficulties that might arise, and to atone for our mistakes by patience.

Far from that, without even desiring war, we began with an absurd outburst. Then we retreated, hoping that Prussia would not too keenly feel our sally, and that England, the usual arbitrator, would arrange all. I interposed to advise prudence and frank acceptance of Prussia's concession, — a concession which was inevitable, that power having put itself in the wrong. My advice was accepted, and all was promised me. At this moment our Government had passed from arrogance to fear, and desired but one thing, — the relinquishment of the Hohenzollern candidature. The anxiously awaited news arrived, and in his joy M. Ollivier hastened to the Chamber. Reaching the lobby at the same moment, I said to him that we ought to be satisfied. "Yes, yes," he replied, "the affair is settled." On the instant the Bonapartists, who think to regain power if the Empire recovers its prestige, set up howls of wrath, not in the Hall of Sessions, but in the lobbies, where all this took place. The outcry was furious. I said to M. Ollivier and his colleagues, "Stand firm ; do not be afraid, and we will back you up." That afternoon a Cabinet Council was held. For war, M. Lebœuf, drunk with ambition ; M. Rigault de Genouilly, hesitating, but finally joining his colleague-at-arms ; and M. de Gramont. The five others were for peace. But the strident voice of the war-party had been heard at the Tuileries. The five men of peace became cowed, and devised a compromise between peace and war ; that is, the requirement of pledges from the King of Prussia. And what pledges ! I straightway told the Ministers that they had at one stroke sacrificed France, humanity, and good policy. They thought not, and promised to be moderate. I persisted in deeming everything lost, and unhappily I was right. Meanwhile, however, the others begged me to place myself at their head, and promised to be very brave.

Alas ! the poor men were incapable of courage ! The famous story of the outrage to France arrived from Berlin ; Ministers and Ministerialists seized upon it, cried that France was insulted, war necessary ; and so the famous sitting of July 15 took place. Upon the reading of the Ollivier Manifesto, there were whoops as of drunken savages ; everybody was terrified. I arose, moved by one of the most unpremeditated impulses that ever sprang from an honest heart. I was greeted with howls of rage ; but, as you saw, I held my ground to the end.

What will come of this accumulation of futilities, weaknesses, and follies, I cannot foretell. We must earnestly desire victory ; but victory, if it saves our territory, will take away our liberty. Our condition is therefore lamentable ; for in any event we have something very precious to lose. I am not disturbed by the storm that has burst upon me ; one cannot be a good citizen at less cost.

The cruel days came apace. How many indifferent ones must have regretted sacrificing the safeguards of a free country, and abandoning themselves ! It was quickly perceived that the warlike preparation, of which so much was made, which seemed the sufficient reason for declaring war, was a mere pitfall. To what end this precipitancy, this unwillingness to listen to any explanation, to communicate any despatch, if not in order to gain some days upon the

surprised Prussians ?   The Emperor himself —
before whom the well-known phrase, "We are
ready!" had been repeated for years, and who,
in spite of a painful disease, felt it necessary to
go to the front — was greatly astonished at not
having to set out at once.   He had prepared
to leave St. Cloud the day after the session,
and his departure was delayed from day to day !
He is said to have been greatly disturbed by
this, and to have remarked to one of those who
accompanied him to the army, " There are mo-
ments when I fear that M. Thiers was right."

M. Thiers was only too much in the right.
He was himself surprised at the condition of
the armament and of the army, when, after
having done everything to avert the war, he
endeavored to give some advice as to its conduct.   He occupied himself with the matter
at first merely by the authority which experience gave him, afterward officially.   The
circumstances of his taking office are little
known.   On the 18th of August, the Empress
intrusted M. Mérimée — who was already
suffering with the malady of which he was
so soon to die — with a delicate negotiation.
She wished to see M. Thiers, to ask his advice and assistance, — about what, she did not
say, — and she promised him her entire confidence.   Thiers kindly and firmly refused.

"Why should I see her? This is calling a physician when the case has become desperate!"

"But what if she should publicly summon you?"

"I could not refuse to obey, but my language would be the same; and such a fruitless step would only advertise our extremity without alleviating it. My conditions would be such as these: the abdication of the Emperor; the concentration of our forces at Paris; the decision to fight the decisive battle under the shadow of the fortifications, and to arm the whole population. Even then I could not promise to attempt a desperate enterprise without knowing what resources I might have at my disposal."

What especially struck Thiers in the conversation was that Mérimée did not blench at the word "abdication." To such a pass had the most devoted friends of the Imperial régime been brought in the course of a few days! That evening a note from Mérimée informed Thiers that the Empress understood his motives, and desired only that he should be assured that she had thought of him in perfect good faith. She did not, however, give up her plan. A renewed negotiation was undertaken by Prince Richard de Metternich, the result of which was that M. Thiers was by decree appointed a member of the Council of Defence. Still he would not accept, unless the nomination was confirmed by the Corps Législatif. This confirmation was made by acclamation. He whom they had insulted, a month earlier, as a false prophet, whom they would willingly have stoned as a traitor, now saw his greatest foes bow before his authority, implore his advice, question him as an oracle. The whole nation seemed to look for help to him alone.

Fresh chagrins and struggles awaited him in this Council. He saw the wretchedness that was hidden under the Imperial purple; he opposed, with passionate urgency, the measures that deprived Paris of its garrison, and the movement of Marshal MacMahon which was to end in the disaster of Sedan. Seeing the inutility of his efforts. he was a hundred times on the point of resigning; but this would have weakened the defence, and he stood at his post to the end. When, after the defeat, the Emperor's dethronement was called for in the Corps Législatif, Thiers' moderation led him to propose a softer word, that of a "vacancy of the throne," in order to spare the dignity of those who had not spared his. Instead of immediately discussing this and other propositions, the Chamber stood upon form, and the deputies, not perceiving that time pressed, retired to the committee-rooms.

Meantime the news of the disaster spread outside, and the public crowded toward the Chamber. In his deposition before the Committee of Inquiry, Sept. 17, 1871, Thiers described the situation as follows: —

" The Empire had aroused such indignation by the woes it had brought upon the land, that no one felt sorry for its fall or thought of keeping it in power. Its own partisans took part, without resistance, in this singular scene. Those partisans of the Empire, so dejected then, are on their feet again to-day, complaining of their overthrow, alleging that France was smitten in their person. But why did they not then resist? Why did they not make a single effort to impede that spontaneous Revolution? For a good reason : because there was not a single person, even among them, who dreamed of saving the Empire. Violence there was none. The deputies walked about, mingling with a crowd of well-dressed people, who addressed us by name, and kept repeating to me, ' Monsieur Thiers, get us out of this ! ' "

CHAPTER VI.

THE WAR.

THE Republic was proclaimed by the masses without resistance. From the 4th of September the Government was extinct. It was hardly a revolution, — the public merely accepted facts as they stood. That these facts were not regularly established is, however, to be regretted. Though the Corps Législatif had hardly any more right than any other concourse of citizens to fix upon a course of action, nevertheless it should have been permitted to appoint a Government' of National Defence and to convoke the electors. But hardly any one thought of such a thing. The deputies of Paris accepted summary investiture from the multitude and dissolved the Corps Législatif. Thiers could not consent to take part in a Government thus improvised, but he did not think the Corps Législatif in a position to interfere. In a sitting held that same evening in one of the halls of the Bourbon Palace, he confined himself to remarking with some irony that it was not for the servants of the Empire to invoke the sanctity of the popular mandate, and that every one would do well to forget all but the defence of the national soil. This was his first and sole preoccupation.

The proclamation of the Republic was a surprise to no one. For a long time past it had been impossible for any one to think that any other Government could succeed the Empire. Could this Government immediately make peace? It would have been very desirable to leave the whole responsibility for our sufferings with the Emperor. But the enemy, after his first successes, had determined not to retire empty-handed; and any one who had at that time suggested a treaty involving the cession of Strasburg, the defence of which still continued, would have been deemed a coward or insane. No signatures at the foot of a diplomatic paper would have availed against the popular wrath. Even those whose forebodings of the future were gloomiest did not for a moment think of laying down their arms. Moreover, Paris still remained, — Paris fortified by the efforts of Thiers, Paris which, from being the revolutionary capital of France, might and should be transformed into its citadel; and men loved to think that so long as Paris was ours, France could not be regarded as conquered. It was to the preparations for this defence that Thiers now expected to devote himself.

This austere and modest dream was broken by a visit from M. Jules Favre, Minister of Foreign Affairs, who proposed to Thiers a mission abroad. The entire Government, including M. Rochefort, requested him to visit the principal cabinets of Europe, and to urge upon them the reasons why they could not afford to allow the equilibrium of the world to be overset by the fall of France and by the menace of a universal monarchy. Could he not awaken in some quarters the remembrance of services rendered, inform the nations concerning the state of France, prove that she was not destined to perish, favorably represent the new Republic, obtain the goodwill and even the support of neutral powers ? His antecedents, his fame, his energetic opposition to the war, his knowledge of politics and of men, marked him out as the only man capable of undertaking such a mission. Notwithstanding his seventy-three years, notwithstanding his wish and his right to have nothing to do with a war so wrongly undertaken, he decided to accept. To represent a suppliant and defeated France after having for a lifetime desired to see her strong and proud, after having enhanced and celebrated her military glory, was very painful. But he gave himself wholly to the stricken land, unmindful that she might again prove ungrateful.

There was no time to hesitate. The very next day Paris was to be shut in, and behind the train that carried him to Calais on the 12th of September, the engineers blew up Creil bridge in order to delay the march of the Prussians. He began with England. The English, in whom coldness is no sign of ill-will, were gradually becoming favorable to us. Thiers found this friendly feeling very marked among the people of all nations. Everywhere, in the railway-stations, in the streets, in the hotels, touching evidences of fellowship appeared in men's words, in their faces, in their eyes often filled with tears; and thus the bitterness of the journey was mitigated. Governments were not blind to this popular sympathy, and refusals which wrung the heart were couched in the kindest terms. This amenity could not have been more perfectly felt and expressed than by Her Majesty's amiable Minister of Foreign Affairs. Lord Granville, so French in turn of mind, in tastes and habits, received Thiers as a friend. But neither he

nor Mr. Gladstone would make any promises
that they could not keep. Of armed intervention on the part of England there could
be no question, but only of good offices; and
even in these the English deemed it not wise
to take the initiative. But they promised to
recognize the new Government as soon as
an Assembly could be convoked to give it a
legal existence. This had been their custom
after each one of our revolutions, even that of
December 2d (1851); and as the Imperial
policy had never given them any security,
they had no especial reason to regret the 4th
of September. The opinion of the British
Cabinet was that any initiative must proceed
from Russia; and they felt that if Tsar Alexander were to pronounce favorably, they might
themselves venture upon something more than
fair words. This was not only the opinion of
the English, but also that of the Russian Ambassador, M. de Brunnow, an astute old gen-
tleman well disposed toward us, who believed
that a visit from Thiers would effect wonders
with Prince Gortschakoff and the Tsar.

From London to St. Petersburg the way is
long. The sea was patrolled by German ships
which would have liked to capture an important emissary; and even had he escaped them,
how could he pass a week without news from

home, and reach Russia absolutely ignorant
of the situation? On the other hand, the land
journey around Prussia was difficult; but it was
upon this that he decided. A light ship had
been sent him, — the same that Prince Napoleon had used for his voyages. The passage
from London to Cherbourg was made in twenty-
four hours, and he immediately took the train
for Tours, where he arrived somewhat behind
time the next morning. The preceding train
had suffered the serious accident, near Mettray,
wherein several persons perished, — notably
M. Jules Duval, the well-known editor of the
" Journal des Débats."

In a few hours Thiers was informed touching the military situation by Admiral Fourrichon, Minister of War. Paris was not entirely
blockaded, but the Prussians were constantly
advancing, without meeting any serious resistance. Even with the French Ministers, Thiers
did not forget his mission. It was almost as
difficult to convince them of the necessity of
convoking an Assembly, as to prevail upon
foreign governments to preserve the European
balance of power. They acceded, however, to
the plan of elections for the 2d of October, —
elections which were so often to be postponed;
and Thiers set out again in the afternoon in
the hope of soon representing, not merely a

government born of a popular uprising, but an Assembly based upon universal suffrage.

Station after station flashed by the rushing train; at the least halt the whole population crowded about to ask the news, to relate their sorrows, to express their hopes for the success of the mission. Thiers' emotion was such that he was sometimes unable to reply. The next day the frontier was passed, and after crossing Mont Cenis, — for the tunnel was not completed, — he set foot upon Italian soil. The little town of Susa, which he reached Wednesday, September 21, at seven o'clock in the evening, was in gala array, and, a little later, illuminated. For the Italian troops had entered Rome! That day Italian unity had been achieved without a conflict and almost without a blow. The Italians exhibited none the less demonstrative sympathy for France and for her envoy. This was, however, no time to ask Victor Emmanuel's Ministers for political or military support. So Thiers did not stop at Turin, at Milan, at Venice, or at Nabresina, but went straight through to Vienna, where he had an interview with Count von Beust, Chancellor of the Austro-Hungarian Empire. This conversation, and that upon Thiers' return, are related by Beust in his agreeable "Memoirs." It was hardly to be expected that Austria, conquered by us in 1859 and by Prussia in 1866, would be much disposed to meddle in the bloody struggle of her two adversaries. Nevertheless, Minister Gramont, in the sitting of July 15, had said or implied that France might count upon an Austrian alliance. The Chancellor had no difficulty in showing that nothing, either in his words or in his despatches, had authorized such an assertion, and that he had done everything to explain this to the minister. He afterward stated the same thing in print. But he was no enemy of a country to which he was allied by the graces of his mind, and he lamented his powerlessness. He expressed his regrets to Thiers, adding that the latter would receive throughout Europe, and especially in Italy, fair words and nothing more. "Oh!" said Thiers sadly, "I have not been spoiled!"[1] The Austrians were very hostile to the fallen Emperor. In the lively streets of the handsome city was everywhere to be seen a caricature representing Napoleon kneeling repentant before Thiers, who, in the character of the Pythoness, was saying: "Wretch! did I not tell you that there was not a blunder left to be committed?"

He made the run of sixty hours from Vienna to St. Petersburg without stopping. He was

[1] Memoire du comte de Beust, iii. 350.

in haste to see Prince Gortschakoff, who
seemed to hold the key of the situation. The
latter had indeed spoken in no very assuring
manner to M. de Saint-Vallier on the day of
the Gramont declaration. But times were
changed; France was no longer that haughty
and mischief-making Empire whose humiliation was seen without regret; and even those
who did not pity our misfortunes might be disturbed by the success of a power no less dangerous and turbulent. In default of material
support, Thiers felt that Russia would at least
entertain a sincere desire for peace. The
Chancellor could not be insensible to the com-
pliment paid him in this long journey. Every
diplomatist is by nature or art something of a
Frenchman, and none can be insensible to
the advantage of pleasing a distinguished
Frenchman. Moreover, Thiers was not simply
making this journey in his own name; he represented the Republic, and the sentiments of
this government were to be inferred from its
choice of an Ambassador. France's strength
was still considerable and its resistance still
vigorous. The inhabitants of Paris were con-
ducting themselves like heroic soldiers in a
beleaguered citadel. Would not Prince Gortschakoff be tempted to aid in this uprising
of a great nation, and to countenance some

measure leading to a truce and to the formation of an Assembly, either in order to resume relations upon a securer basis, or in order to bring about a treaty which was desired by neutrals and was perhaps necessary to the belligerents, and which might result in a peace of some solidity? The Tsar would have no objections, and whatever might have been said, would not hesitate to treat with the Republic. He had little regret for Napoleon III., to whom he attributed the disagreeable incidents of his visit to Paris in 1867. Provided that the Government which was to succeed were peaceable and lasting, the Tsar would not too closely scrutinize the etiquette of the arrangement. At bottom, all the sovereigns of Europe think of France as a Republic for the last hundred years.

Thiers discussed the means and the end in several interviews, which resulted in the Tsar's offer to write personally to the king of Prussia, asking him to authorize M. Thiers to repair to his headquarters and to treat for an armistice intended to facilitate the election of an Assembly. This was accepted, subject of course to the consent of the French Government, which could be obtained only at Tours and at Paris.

Again Thiers had to cross those broad, silent steppes and to traverse Poland, whose affection for France was so touching. At

Vienna, he found Count Beust still of the same opinion. At Florence, he had an interview with King Victor Emmanuel, whom he found extremely French in manner, in conversation, and in heart, but restrained by his subjects and by his Parliament. The king had also conceived a plan of peaceable intervention, and had imparted it to the British Cabinet, which, even before the Tsar's despatch passed over the wires, had proposed to the neutral powers a common intervention. Thus four powers advised the Armistice, and Bismarck accepted the negotiation.

Thiers now had only to return to Tours in order to confer with the Delegation. This he did forthwith. A change had taken place in his mind: in the first days of the war he put away all thought of participation in this cruel peace; he felt that he had no right to attach his name to any of the results of an enterprise he had so urgently opposed. Little by little he came to feel that peace would be a relative good, and would put an end to these terrible calamities. His imagination grew familiar with the thought of employing his credit in Europe for the deliverance of his country, which, thanks to his efforts, might have to pay a smaller price for peace. But on his return to France he found a different disposition; or rather he had been sent out from Paris by the peace party, and now had to negotiate at Tours with the war party. M. Gambetta, full of generous illusions, was imparting his own fire to a great number of the citizens and of the army; and this he could not do without holding out the hope of victory, without seeking to inspire a horror of the sacrifices which must be the price of peace. The violence of his proclamations, perhaps inevitable in the circumstances, seemed to render impossible the opening of a negotiation. But beneath Gambetta's declamation was concealed a sagacious and sensible mind. He understood the necessity for the proposed step, though he wished that it might not succeed, and that a chance might still be left for delivering France by force of arms. Finally, on the 28th of October, Thiers was able to leave Tours for Paris by way of Versailles, the seat of the German headquarters. This journey was still more painful than that from which he had just returned, since it was necessary to cross our devastated fields under the escort of the invaders.

It was in the Bishop of Orleans' pastoral coach, drawn by German artillery teams, that the negotiator, after two days' journey, reached Versailles, where, as at Orleans, great placards in the German language announced the sur-

render of Marshal Bazaine and enumerated the
number of cannon captured and the number of
French soldiers sent to Germany. The number of the latter reached four hundred thousand! Such a success could not but render
our conquerors terribly exacting, not as to
their territorial claims, which had from the time
of their first victories been excessive, but as
to the other conditions of the Armistice. If the
Government at Paris would, like the Delegation at Tours, authorize negotiations looking
toward this Armistice, several considerations
might determine the Prussians to accept it.
First, willingness to satisfy the neutral powers,
which, either through humanity or through
policy, desired the end of the war; secondly,
the advantage to the victors themselves of
having to do with a recognized Government
capable of negotiating in the name of France
and of putting an end to the siege of Paris;
thirdly, the well-grounded fear of the new
armies which were everywhere forming;
fourthly, the very serious dissensions among
the confederated German nations, some of
which did not conceal their desire for peace.
But the best argument of the negotiator would
still have been the resistance of Metz, where
our best troops had kept a whole German
army-corps from moving.

On reaching Versailles, Thiers had nothing to do but obtain from Bismarck permission to pass the outposts and enter Paris. Bismarck understood that there could be no negotiation until the powers of the negotiator had been confirmed by the Government, for the Ministers at Tours were only a Delegation. " We shall discuss matters upon your return, if you return," said Bismarck; "for we are informed that a new revolution is brewing at Paris, and there may be danger in your going there."

The trip from Versailles to Sèvres was made in the same carriage, which the Prussian officer halted at the head of the Grande-Rue. He informed M. Thiers that he was about to descend in order to make the necessary signals to stop a firing which was doing no great harm, but was making a great deal of noise. This street of Sèvres was especially exposed to the bombs of Mt. Valérien. " You will have to wait a little while," said the officer, " until the signals are understood and the firing entirely ceases." " In France," replied Thiers, gallantly, " we make no difference as to courage between soldiers and civilians; " and he descended to the high bank of the Seine. Soon a boat manned by a single French soldier pushed off from the opposite bank and crossed the river, — for Sèvres bridge had been destroyed. As the little red-trousered infantry-man coolly rowed them across, while the bombs shrieked above their heads, Thiers said to his companion, who held the tiller, "Do you know what I should call the picturesque in history? The crushing by a French bomb of this skiff which bears deliverance and peace to the Parisians!"

Thiers was greatly moved upon entering Paris, as were those who received him and heard from his lips the news from the rest of France. The whole evening, almost the whole night, was passed in conversations which resulted in the acceptance of the Armistice on the part of the Paris Government. The capital had gloriously resisted. In the opinion of those who had fortified it in 1840, Paris was not a citadel intended to defend itself to the last morsel of bread, but rather a vast intrenched camp suited to serve as a shelter to an army. But army there was none. At the decisive moment Marshal MacMahon had marched into the ambush at Sedan, instead of retiring under the walls of the capital. Paris could never raise the siege herself, the army at Metz had just been lost, and it was almost demonstrated that the soldiers of the provinces, though they might gain some isolated advantages, would never be able to break the iron band that encompassed Paris for thirty leagues. How could a wise Government have refused the Armistice which, without any weak concession on the part of the besieged, leaving matters *in statu quo*, would permit France and even Paris to elect deputies and thus to be regularly represented? If, then, the war should be continued, the capital would be a little refreshed for her courageous sacrifice, the provincial conscripts would have had a month in which to drill, sympathetic Europe would have become more interested in us, and the German Confederates would have had an opportunity to quarrel.

It was evident very early the following morning that the population of Paris was aroused and irritated. In the evening we had suffered a reverse at the village of Bourget, after a success the importance of which had been exaggerated; and now the cry of treason was raised, — the usual resource of vanity. The capitulation of Metz, having been announced by a newspaper before it occurred, had been very properly denied by the Minister, who was now compelled to publish it, and was therefore accused of falsehood. Wild rumors of the negotiation circulated through the crowds of people enervated by the sufferings of the siege. There was evidently to be what the Parisians call a *day* (*journée*), — the 31st of October, — and Thiers ran a serious risk of realizing Bismarck's prediction, and of becoming a prisoner of the mob rather than of the enemy. This would have been awkward for the negotiation; and since, after all, the Government seemed capable of putting down the insurrection, since all was agreed upon, since it was important to put an end to all these painful scenes, since he could at any time return, he determined to proceed at once to Versailles.

Bismarck did not peremptorily refuse Thiers' propositions, but entered into the discussion of details, not always in his own name, but in the name of the military party, and of the king, whom he represented as more exacting than himself. The greatest difficulty was that of the revictualling. An Armistice of a month, with the exclusion of supplies from Paris, would have been equivalent to another month of siege, and the conclusion of it would find us weaker than at the beginning. If, on the contrary, cattle and vegetables were shipped to the capital, such a month of repose would be a great advantage to us. This was the principal point at issue; for Thiers was bound to resist the wiles of the Chancellor, who was ready to yield much if his interlocutor would treat of definitive peace. "You are a publisher of books," said he to Thiers, "and I am quite willing to treat with you concerning the first volume, the Armistice, if you can promise me the second, which is Peace." Thiers had no right to undertake this second negotiation; he was invested with no real power. He was merely intrusted with a very special mission by the Government of the National Defence, which itself had no ulterior powers.

On the other hand, it was but natural that Bismarck should wish to profit by his interviews with a man so considerable, to go beyond this, and to prepare at least the groundwork of a treaty. In spite of so many victories, — by reason of them indeed, — this treaty appeared a difficult one to conclude, and the Chancellor foresaw great perplexities in the task of reconciling the claims of the Prussian military party with the just pride of the French people. It was to be expected that our misfortunes would abate this pride; but at that time this remarkable saying of Bismarck was quoted. "All this is very fine, is it not?" said he to a German general after Sedan, "but it will make peace very difficult!" It was to almost the same effect that Victor Hugo afterward said: " Henceforward there will be two formidable nations, — the one because victorious, the other because vanquished."

Three days had passed in discussions which seemed about to terminate, when on Thursday Bismarck seemed less inclined to treat, and said abruptly to Thiers: "Are you sure that you represent even the Revolutionary Government of the Defence? The report comes from the outposts that a new revolution took place at Paris on the 31st of October, that the Jacobin party was victorious, and that the Government of the National Defence is overthrown. Have I the honor to treat with the representative of M. Félix Pyat and his friends?"

Disturbed by this unforeseen and tardy communication, Thiers obtained authorization from the Chancellor to send to Paris for authentic information. He then learned that the Ministry presided over by General Trochu had been captured at the Hôtel de Ville, and afterward delivered by the courage and presence of mind of Messrs. Picard and Ferry. The next day this Government submitted its claims to a kind of plebiscite. The powers of the Government of Defence were indeed confirmed, but only after a promise to entertain no propositions of peace.

Although the news still justified Thiers in negotiating, his authority was sensibly diminished, and the more since a proclamation very hostile to peace and even to negotiation emanated at the same juncture from Gambetta. All this made the Prussians more arrogant. Not only would they not concede the necessary quantity of provisions, but they demanded the surrender of a fort as a pledge of good faith. To give up a fort was to give up Paris at the termination of the Armistice, in case peace should not then be concluded. A Government might subscribe to such a condition, but a negotiator scarcely assured of his powers was bound to refuse even to discuss it. Thiers therefore claimed the right to refer the matter to the Paris Government. " I consent," said Bismarck, " but more than last week you run the risk of being detained; and you ask of us a great sacrifice, for they pay less and less attention, at Paris, to the trumpet and the flag of truce; each letter costs us a man." All risks were, however, to be taken in the interests of a negotiation that might check further bloodshed. Thiers returned to Paris by way of Sèvres; but the Ministers, fearing a new tumult, gave him rendezvous at Billancourt. There, in an abandoned house, he found M. Jules Favre and General Ducrot. Both, especially the latter, declared that neither the Government nor the City, at best scarcely favorable to a clearly advantageous armistice, could entertain a thought of the proposed one, the inevitable upshot of which would be peace. The Government therefore begged M. Thiers to throw up the negotiation and to leave the German headquarters.

He again made his way to Versailles and then to Tours, whence he sent to the neutral powers an account of his mission in a despatch which has been published. He could now do nothing but watch the course of events with anxiety, for he placed little trust in Gambetta's improvised armies, officered as they were by novices, the experienced officers being for the most part prisoners in Germany. Under the Empire, the effective strength of the regiments had been so slight that an undue proportion of officers had been sent to the front. As Thiers put it, "they had undertaken to wage war with *cadres*."

No considerable success came to give lustre to our arms. That unbroken line of defeats and disasters gave the lie to all the common-places about the inconstancy of Fortune. Paris, noble Paris, so guilty in other days, now alone sometimes gave us those thrills of patriotic joy which had once seemed to us the necessary accompaniment of every war. But the capital saved naught but her honor, and when, in January, 1871, she was obliged by starvation to surrender, all hope disappeared with her. The Government was obliged to treat, not only for the city but for all France, and to agree to a truce for the election of deputies.

The elections passed off more quietly than was to be expected, and the Assembly which came together at Bordeaux on the 13th of February, exactly represented the sentiment of the nation at that particular moment. France being eager for peace, the Assembly was pacific. It was also somewhat unrepublican, for the Republic had been represented in the provinces only by Gambetta, the promoter of war to the knife, who had sacrificed the interests of the Republic to what he conceived to be the interests of the national honor. Politics had, in truth, been little thought of, and Thiers was elected in twenty-seven departments upon very diverse tickets, rather on account of his opposition to the war and his efforts in favor of peace than on account of his fame as a liberal orator and historian. Moved by the same impulse, the Assembly almost unanimously appointed him Chief of the Executive Power of the French Republic, and intrusted to him the double task of governing the country and of treating with the German Emperor.

Thus began a new phase of his restless existence. Fate bestowed upon him in the decline of life the highest fortune, and the opportunity to display his rarest powers in the performance of new services to his country.

CHAPTER VII.

THE THIRD REPUBLIC.

"DERIVING authority from his capacity and acknowledged worth, being also a man of transparent integrity, Pericles was able to control the multitude in a free spirit; he led them rather than was led by them; for, not seeking power by dishonest arts, he had no need to say pleasant things, but, on the strength of his own high character, could venture to oppose and even to anger them. When he saw them unseasonably elated and arrogant, his words humbled and awed them; and when they were depressed by groundless fears, he sought to reanimate their confidence. Thus Athens, though still in name a democracy, was in fact ruled by her greatest citizen."[1]

These words may be taken as a faithful expression of Thiers' historic character as Chief Magistrate. He was really our first citizen, and it was as such that he was asked to discuss terms of peace with Bismarck, — "that barbarian of genius," as Thiers called

[1] Thucydides, ii. lxv. Jowett's version.

him. It is well known what efforts Thiers was compelled to make in order to preserve to France the city of Belfort, which had been singled out in advance as German prey. It is also matter of history how this inevitable and painful peace was ratified by the Assembly, after one of the most touching speeches ever pronounced by a patriot.

It was apparently in the name of the Republic that peace was negotiated and the Government gradually reconstructed. This Government had been proclaimed on the 4th of September; in its name Gambetta had raised armies and convoked electors; and Thiers, when proclaimed Chief of the Executive Power, had, at the instance of M. Dufaure, who made this the condition of accepting a portfolio, desired that the title should read, " Chief of the Executive Power *of the French Republic.*" Moreover, in the nature of things, as Molière observes, whatever is not prose is verse, — where there is neither king nor emperor there must be a republic. The Assembly, however, which was all-powerful, held that to change the form of government was one of its rights. It might have been urged that the electors had scarcely contemplated this, and that the Monarchists were in the majority simply because they represented peace, while in the provinces the Republic had meant nothing but war to the hilt. But these distinctions were not thought of in the press of more urgent business, namely, the treaty which was to check the shedding of blood, and the rudiments of administrative reconstruction. No monarchy would have been willing to assume the responsibility of this Treaty; this the Monarchical Right thoroughly understood. The Right accordingly consented to accept the name of Republic as a makeshift, provided it should be talked about as little as possible.

Thiers had come to think, especially since the beginning of the war, that the Republic was the natural heir of Napoleon III., and that it would at last be necessary to cross the ocean rather than the Channel. He saw that here only would a conservative policy find a solid groundwork whereon to build. He had, however, been struck with the circumstance that so many Legitimists had been elected to the Assembly, and he was no more eager than they to stop to discuss constitutions when the Treaty was to be ratified and Paris, whence there came very alarming news, to be pacified. He was the more disposed to wait, inasmuch as he saw in the Chamber the very rapid formation and growth of a group in which he had great confidence. Of these deputies M. Jules Simon has given a better definition than they could themselves formulate, — for this political philosopher has written a masterly history of these years.[1] Differing with Thiers upon many points of constitutional theory or social economy, M. Simon was like him in three things that ought to suffice to bind men together, — talent, courage, and zeal for the public welfare. Here is what Simon says of this party in the Assembly: —

"There were in this body some five-score firm spirits who were alike incapable either of forsaking the principles whereon all society rests, or of giving up freedom. Of all forms of government they would have preferred constitutional monarchy, had they found it established, or could they have restored it by a vote without resort to force. But they quickly perceived that neither the Legitimists nor the Bonapartists would consent to the constitutional form ; that such a monarchy could obtain a majority neither in the Parliament nor among the people ; that, both by its nature and by the disposition of its defenders, it would be happily incapable of recourse to violence ; and that the reappearance of the Legitimist party upon the political stage was a passing incident of little significance. Some of these men entertained for the Republic a distrust which, at first, amounted to aversion. Being persuaded, however, that they must choose

[1] Le gouvernement de M. Thiers, par Jules Simon. 2 vols. S⁰, Paris, 1878.

between the Republic and the Empire, and that the latter could never harmonize either with the principles of right and justice or with freedom, they did not despair of forming a Republic at once liberal and conservative. In a word, they thrust aside the Legitimate Monarchy as chimerical, Republican and Cæsarian dictatorship as alike hateful; and while preferring a liberal Monarchy to a moderate Republic, they saw no reason to resort to a revolution merely in order to make the Presidency of the Republic hereditary. Of this party M. Thiers was not merely the head, but the body also."

This party, which was then very willing to realize what had been called the Liberal Union, thought, and still thinks, that republican ideas are merely the maximum of liberal ideas. Unfortunately, however, there are people who take fright at their ideas when they see them carried out. But there was another party which, although the least numerous in the Assembly and split into factions at that, was the most numerous in the country, — the Republican party. What could Thiers do to prevent these parties from " falling upon one another," to quote his own expression? Precisely what he did do, with a consummate art not inconsistent with perfect sincerity. He said to the Royalists, " You have the power of making a Constitution, and it is very reasonable in you to refrain from exercising that power;" to the Republicans, "Peace is concluded, administration is reconstructed, the finances are restored,—all in the name and for the benefit of the Republic; definitive success will be with the most prudent." These things he said, not in secret conclaves, in private conversations, but in the open Assembly, and not once but ten times. His chief care was to reassure the Republicans who might do him the injustice to suspect that, in the capacity of Head of the Republic, he was paving the way to a Restoration. He was thus obliged to promise at every turn that he would not betray the trust confided to him. Betray it to whom? Certainly not to the Monarchy of right divine, which he had always opposed, but rather to a combination midway between Republic and Monarchy,—a species of Orleanist Stadtholdership. This political and moral difficulty was greatly lessened by the conduct of the Orleans princes, who publicly declared that although they might have a *claim*, they had no *right* to govern, and who accepted the Republic to the extent of taking office under it. The chief among them, the Duke of Aumale, served the Republic usefully and nobly. None of them seemed to think that the House of Orleans should be anything more than a House of

Orange, contributing indifferently Revolutionary kings and Republican magistrates.

Thiers set forth his policy to the Assembly at Bordeaux, notably on the 10th of March, 1871, in language so clear and sincere that one is embarrassed to have to explain and justify it. Nevertheless, he found himself obliged to return to the subject more than once, and to repeat words which have received a glorious justification from events. A few hours after delivering this speech he returned to Paris, the Assembly having consented, at his request, to sit at Versailles. He found the capital in great commotion, and his efforts to destroy the last traces of the siege and the germs of civil strife were fruitless. He had neither an armed force, nor a civil administration, nor means of making his voice heard by a restless, irritated, inflamed population. The murders of Generals Lecomte and Clément Thomas were the signals for the setting up of the Commune, which was to end as it had begun. What was to be done against an insurrection that had all the organization, all the resources, of a regular army, — an army made up in large part of disbanded soldiery? Thiers took the bold course which he had on another occasion advised: he transferred the seat of Government to Versailles, whither he betook himself on the eve of the session of the Assembly. The best judges have thought this to be one of the happiest strokes of his practical genius. At all events, the Assembly was able to deliberate in peace, the Commune was put down, and order was restored.

Readers of history who have not seen it in the making, may be surprised to learn that so great an achievement brought about little change in party feeling. The deputies who wished to substitute the Monarchy for the Republic saw in it an encouragement; the rest understood better that an insurrection raised in the name of the Republic could be put down only by the Republic herself. Some members of the Commune may really have thought the Government imperilled by the Monarchical majority in the Assembly. More than ever Thiers was compelled to prove himself no traitor to the Republic. The moderate Republicans were disarmed by his assurances, and if he did not bring over all the opponents of the Empire to his support, he at least compelled all who were not foes of society to range themselves on the side of law. The partisans of authority, who were barely respectful to his authority, held him strictly to account, so that he repeated at Versailles what he had said at Bordeaux, and this with unwearied patience and inexhaustible variety of forms. The following words are from his speech of March 27, 1871 : —

"There exist foes of society who repeat that we are preparing to overthrow the Republic. This I flatly and formally deny. They are deceiving France; their aim is to disturb and arouse the country. We found the Republic already established, a fact of which we were not the authors. But I shall not destroy the form of government of which I now make use in order to restore order."

Some days later, in full tide of war against the Commune, the Assembly decided, by a great majority, that the mayors of all the communes of France should be appointed by the municipal councils. In a time of tranquillity this would have been justifiable; but it was of doubtful wisdom at a juncture when the communes seemed about to rebel against the Central Power, when schemes of decentralization were rife, when decentralization was being carried to an absurd extreme by a faction in the Chamber, and to a criminal extreme by the Commune of Paris. Thiers, who was a firm centralizer, found himself forced to defend the Republic by cannon against the Communists of Paris, and by the tongue against the decentralizers of Versailles. The difference in arms marks the difference in the persons and their aims, but it is interesting to note how persistently men's minds were at that time haunted by such inapplicable or criminal ideas. It is worthy of note, also, that the very persons who urged this democratic method of electing the mayors, reproached Thiers with holding out too much hope to the delegates of the communes and of the great towns.

These delegates, disturbed by the reports current in the provinces of preparations for a Monarchical Restoration, thronged the presidential anterooms. A month of dreadful suspense passed in the fear of a widespread insurrection that could not have been suppressed. This was escaped; but Thiers was compelled to pledge himself still more explicitly to the Republic, and to insist upon the Republican character of the Government. This attitude, the only reasonable and possible one, was becoming easier, for liberal and wise Republicans were beginning to rally loyally to the support of a Government which bore their colors, and by means of which they might hope to escape the still imminent reign of the anarchists. This feeling was shown in the Assembly by the change of the Chief Magistrate's title to that of President of the

Republic. In the interim, however, two great events had taken place: Thiers had restored order at Paris, and the complementary elections of July had sent more than a hundred moderate Republicans to Versailles.

Party strength had shifted, and the will of France had been clearly expressed. Those who had looked forward to the accession of the Count of Chambord saw with consternation the growth of the conviction on the part of the enlightened classes that the Republic, which had been deemed impossible, was alone possible. The Head of this Republic was restoring order, reconstructing the administration, paying the war-contribution, giving to France a degree of freedom and repose which she had perhaps never known, — and all this in the name of that fragile power, the Bordeaux Compact, which was little more than organized anarchy. Meanwhile, whenever a consequence of the President's efforts came to light, the Assembly was chary of its praise, and failed not to take a large portion of the credit to itself, — witness the sittings in which were announced the termination of the siege of Paris, the payment of an instalment of the national ransom, the conclusion of the various treaties, especially of the one which hastened by two years the evacuation of our territory.

France cherishes with sympathetic admiration the memory of this government, the freest that ever existed, founded in the midst of the greatest difficulties by the " first citizen." It would be interesting to forget his purely political rôle in order to speak of the man himself, or rather of all the men that were blended in him, making him so apt for government. M. Léon Say, his colleague and his friend, in an able and thoughtful address at the unveiling of one of the statues of Thiers, called him "a great financier." In this M. Say was indeed the echo of the public voice, but no one is better qualified to judge. Each of Thiers' Ministers might have said as much touching his particular specialty. M. Hector Pessard, in his pleasant memoirs which he modestly calls " My Little Notes " (*Mes Petits Papiers*), has given the story of one of the President's well-filled days, in which Thiers appears occupied with everything, but finding time for intervals of sparkling conversation. He had the gift, so valuable to a ruler, of persuading every one to whom he gave an order or a counsel that the safety of the State depended upon its execution. And there was nothing touching which he did not command or advise. He was not content with commanding, — he followed to the end the execution of his orders. His Ministers

were well-chosen, for he was somewhat vain
of having the most distinguished men about
him, but they were not always sufficient
for his purposes, and his zeal to have a hand
in the business of all departments of the
government knew no bounds. He had an
ascendency over men that is not sufficiently
explained by the superiority of his mind. His
passionate insistence, his pressing urgency, his
iron will, enabled him to carry his points even
with the most obdurate. He overwhelmed
them with a kind of violence, rather than won
them by persuasion. When aroused upon a
subject that interested him, — and when was
he not so? — he made everything subserve
his aim, whether that aim were financial,
administrative, or military.

The political aim was perhaps the one which
he found most difficult to attain, in the As'sem-
bly at least, for the country was devoted to
him. Between the deputies and Thiers there
was from the first a certain antagonism hidden
under apparent harmony. His policy of union
was at bottom the true French policy, the
policy recommended to Catholics and Protes-
tants by Henry IV. after the capture of Paris.
This system is a most opportune one when the
State and society are to be restored in the
teeth of parties; but it is a peculiarly difficult

system in an Assembly, since an Assembly is
by its very nature an arena for parties with their
jealousies and their grudges. Thiers sincerely
believed that his ideas of order and conservation ought to be a sufficient assurance to every
right-minded man; but even these ideas, when
pressed into the service of the Republic,
could scarcely find grace in the eyes of a
Royalist Right. It has been said that his aim
was to carry out the policy of the Right by
means of the Left, but this is a course which
the Conservative party seems least willing to
tolerate. This party, like all parties, often
prefers, in the Chambers if not in public, to
become revolutionary rather than to relinquish
power. It aims at exclusive dominion. Its
honesty is quite compatible with the rancorous intolerance which sometimes converts virtue into fanaticism. It deems itself the only
party upon which a government can rest.
Such was Guizot's theory in his time, and
Thiers had been looked upon with suspicion
for upwards of thirty years because he would
not subscribe to it. Under the Restoration,
Martignac was abandoned because he made
some members of the Left Centre members of
his Ministry. In 1847, the Conservatives of
the Chamber sacrificed the July Monarchy for
a similar reason; and in 1870 they preferred

to risk the war with Germany rather than submit longer to the Ollivier Ministry.

Thiers' services to the conservative cause could not, therefore, win him the support of the opponents of his general policy. The applause of the Left was sufficient to complete the alienation of the Right. It is impossible to satisfy the passionate except by sharing their passions, and Thiers did not share them. There were days when he might have regained everything by speaking evil of the Republic, or by disobliging this or that Republican. He would not do it, and no right-minded person could blame him, for the Republican party behaved, on the whole, very wisely. It was indeed maintained that the Conservatives would be satisfied if he would but " cut off the tail" of this party. " But when the tail is cut off," said Thiers, "some one is always sure to pick it up and make a plume of it."

As President of the Republic, he might have won over some of the opponents of his general policy by means of private conversation. This he sometimes attempted, his house being always open. But, absorbed as he was, how could he give time to the assiduous attentions of a parliamentary leader? He certainly received people amiably; but, without looking closely into the matter, he reckoned upon the

good-will of those who had cheerfully visited
him or respectfully listened to him. He refused to make allowance for wounded susceptibilities, and was inclined to attribute all
censure to half a dozen malcontents. He
habitually yielded to his faculty of seeing his
own ideas with such plainness that any other
view seemed a contemptible absurdity. By
wounding his opponents he often transformed
them into enemies, — even those who were
not definitely hostile to him, but who merely
found it difficult to accept his extreme personal
share in a parliamentary government. If, as
has been asserted, it was a dictatorship, it was
at least based upon persuasion. He was, however, reproached with being, like Napoleon,
not open to suggestions. This accusation he
seems to have anticipated when he said in his
speech of April 16, 1835: "When a man is in
such a position as to hear the truth only from
those who have the courage to speak it, he
hears it from very few people."

But this President so absolute, so rude at
times, had only to ascend the Tribune to
become a model of simple grace, and to find
a tone of persuasive sincerity which disarmed
or embarrassed his enemies. If at times he
gave way to his temper, he frightened them;
for the Assembly was swayed by the profound

conviction that he was a necessary man, first until the Insurrection was subdued, afterward until the territory was delivered. He had only to threaten to lay down his authority, in order to make everything bend before him. It is therefore comprehensible, if not excusable, that when the Assembly came to undertake the task of framing a Constitution, the first article of this Constitution was that they should close their ears to the charmer, and that Thiers should be, as far as possible, barred out of the French Tribune.

It is not easy to forget the sight of that old man, worn by the toil of night and day, walking up from the President's Palace with his alert step; making his way to the front bench of that theatre glittering with mirrors and gold; sitting there muffled in cloaks, which were rendered necessary by his liability to be chilled by the drafts of that airy hall; listening with a somewhat bantering mien to the speech of some deputy; then suddenly becoming aroused, obtaining the floor, and throwing off with a quick gesture the wraps that impeded the freedom of his movements. Never has modern society, in its nobly democratic phase, been better represented. And then, placing both hands upon the front of the Tribune, he would begin an exposition of his policy of

common-sense, or a course of instruction concerning the finances, the bank, the customs,
the army, while now and then from this unpromising soil would spring, naturally and
unexpectedly, some exquisite flower of Attic
eloquence. The following passage, for example, occurs in the middle of a three hours'
speech on recruitment (June 8, 1872), which
contains more than one bit worthy to be
quoted by the future historian: —

"Take the honest man in our society. Upon attaining manhood he takes a mate and becomes a
father. What is his chief care? I speak of the
honest man. It is by steady, skilful, honest toil to
secure the welfare of his wife, his children, and himself; and not merely present but future welfare. Such
is the honest man. Sometimes even, if he sees a
neighboring family in distress, he will manage to
take something from the comfort of his own children in order to relieve the unfortunate. He is
very rarely in the presence of death, except in his
last hours.

"So much for the life of an honest man in our
society. Now let me show you a very different
society. You take from our fields men who have not
shared in our education, who have not been nourished
upon all the grandeurs of history, who have not lived
with the works and the memories of the Turennes,
the Condés, the Vaubans, the Cæsars, the Hanni-
bals; and to these men you say: 'You are not to

think of your personal welfare. While all around you
is peace, it is the duty of society to keep up your
strength by sufficient food, and not to expose you to
needless dangers. But peace is to be merely an
accident in your existence; in case of need you are
to endure frost and heat, to fling yourselves into the
icy flood of the Beresina, and, when there remains
scarcely a hope of saving the army, you shall still die
to save it. You shall endure the burning heat of
Africa, and your honor, your glory, shall be to die
beneath the flag.'

" Is this the ordinary life of the honest man? No,
it is a life apart, this soldier's life to which our institutions compel certain men. This, gentlemen, is the
school of the soldier. To learn to suffer, to bear in-
tolerable hardships ; to have always before one's eyes
the idea of death ; to be almost happy, when the
moment of danger arrives, to march beside one's
leaders under the flag; and, when that flag is victorious, to triumph, to be glad, glad as with a personal
happiness, — such is the soldier's life."

In a message to the Assembly after the recess of 1872, Thiers made the most complete exposition of his policy. What he had
scarcely ventured to hope for at Bordeaux
had been realized. In less than two years he
had dressed and healed the country's wounds,
and he now presented to the Assembly a nation
peaceful, prosperous, and free. All events and
all elections had declared in favor of a Re-

public. In his turn Thiers now declared for
it, without, however, proposing a Constitution.
It was neither through want of logic nor
through timidity and indecision that he refrained from taking this step, but through a
feeling which was appreciated by very few of
his hearers. At that very moment he was
negotiating with Germany for the anticipated
deliverance of our territory, and he feared to
embarrass the negotiations by the spectacle of
a divided Assembly, incapable of founding a
government, and too much inclined to overthrow him whose individual word was the sole
guarantee in all dealings with foreign governments. He therefore confined himself to sow-
ing his ideas in the minds of men, hoping that
the Assembly would see for itself that the
time had at last come to emerge from this
provisional régime, which was growing unen-
durable. He got no thanks for his discretion.
He was violently attacked, his adversaries being as angry with him for showing that the
Republic was the only government possible as
if he had tried to impose that government by
force. They invoked the famous Bordeaux
Compact, which he had been precisely the one
to respect; for they really could not reproach
him for having governed well, and it was only
by misgovernment that he could have wronged

the Republic. This, indeed, was what discomfited them; they would have been glad of an excuse for a savior of the country, and were vexed to find the country already saved by this eloquent and politic commoner, who, like the great majority of the French middle class, had been made a Republican by reflection.

The Assembly resumed the discussion of fragments of constitutions, of ways and means of organizing, not the Republic, but " Republican government," according to the wire-drawn euphemism of the time. With these debates Thiers had little to do; during the last months of his firm but precarious rule he seldom appeared in the Tribune. The negotiations with Germany took up all his time, and he hastened the liberation with as much eagerness as if the conclusion of the treaty was not to be the signal for a final, victorious attack upon him.

Finally, on the 17th of March, 1873, M. de Rémusat, the Minister of Foreign Affairs, read the Treaty, whereupon the Assembly adjourned for a recess of two months. During this recess the situation was modified by two noteworthy occurrences: the election at Paris of M. Barodet against the Minister of Foreign Affairs, indicating a split in the Republican party; and the declaration by M. Jules Simon in a public speech, that Thiers had delivered the French territory. It is easy to understand what irritation such an assertion must have aroused in certain quarters of the Assembly; while the manifestation on the part of the Parisians, subject though they are to electoral caprices, showed that Thiers could not count upon the support of all shades of Republicans. This was an added reason why the Conservatives should have defended him. The Chamber thought differently, and the resignation of Jules Simon was not deemed a sufficient satisfaction to those who had been wounded by his words. An interpellation signed by three hundred and twenty deputies was made at the opening session, and the 23d of May was fixed upon for the discussion.

The debate lasted for two days, and closed with one of Thiers' finest speeches. He was not eager to retain office, and seemed to think only of justifying his course and of retiring with honor. He made a proud and dignified sketch of his policy. The tone was not provoking, but the underlying ideas were not of a nature to soothe the rancorous and win over the wavering. It was a farewell discourse. To an interrupter he loftily replied: "No! I do not fear for my memory, for I shall not be tried before the tribunal of parties; before them I should be found wanting. But I shall not be condemned at the bar of history, and to that tribunal I appeal."

By a majority of fourteen the Assembly voted an order of the day which Thiers did not approve. He might, however, have retained the Presidency, — for that same Assembly had passed a singular bill enacting that the Chamber and the President should have equal terms and should disappear together. But to what purpose? How could he direct a policy which he deemed bad and dangerous? Collisions would have become more and more frequent and disastrous. He therefore offered his resignation, which was immediately accepted, and France ceased to be governed by the man who had ruled by the divine right of superior intelligence, — a legitimacy as good as any.

CHAPTER VIII.

RETIREMENT AND DEATH.

THIERS' personal friends, who were chiefly concerned about his health and his good name, were in no wise depressed by the parliamentary *coup d'état* that deprived him of power. He gained more in the national respect than he lost in authority. He had great need of rest, and he could not have held out long under the double burden of his seventy-six years and of that overcharged life in which he spared himself neither by day nor by night. It was not, however, to the pleasures of idleness that he gave himself up; his new-found leisure was devoted to his "beloved studies." This expression has been so much abused in France as to have become a mere newspaper commonplace. But Thiers was not acquainted with commonplace: it was a thing that did not exist for him. What he said rendered his impression, his thought; and he employed the right word, careless of what others might associate with that word. He was quite sincere in his delight at the thought of once more working for himself. He was not attached to power for power's sake, but for the sake of carrying out in action the conceptions of his mind. Those who thought otherwise never saw him on one of those days when he threw off the cares of State and permitted himself to indulge his artistic taste and his love of research. They knew nothing of his unaffected pleasure at finding himself once more surrounded by his books, his collections, his unfinished works, — that other life so foreign to the duties of the Head of a State where everything was to be done, to be undone, or to be done over again.

The first part of his retirement was spent in supervising the work upon the house where he intended to pass the remainder of his days. This house in St. George Place had been destroyed by the Commune, and the Assembly had ordered its reconstruction at the expense of the State. But the Assembly could not restore to him the works of art with which his house had been adorned. Before leaving Paris on the 12th of September, 1870, he had, in anticipation of the siege, secured a portion of the collections in the midst of which he had lived for so many years. All that he had been forced to leave was sent by the Communal

Council to the furniture storehouse, and afterward to the Tuileries. Thus the pictures and the marbles that had been the delight of his hours of leisure were consumed with the palace of the sovereigns whose adviser or antagonist he had been, and whose supreme power had fallen to him in the decline of life! He caused the ashes of the palace, and the old curiosity shops, to be searched for the precious remains. All was not consumed; the agents of the Commune had reserved some exquisite bits which were found and repurchased. Artists were employed to restore others; and two years after the 24th of May (1873), Thiers found himself again in a house like the one he had lived in for forty years. Here he took up the thread of the old life, with its amusements and its labors. At five o'clock every morning he was at work in that very private cabinet, where he was surrounded by the beautiful in all its forms, from the celebrated Dancing Mime bought at the Denon sale and the Faun of Praxiteles, to those expressive heads of mules in bronze, which are said to have decorated the chair of the Cæsars. There too were casts of the Farnese Hercules, of Colleone's equestrian statue, of Rude's Mercury, of Cellini's Perseus, and of Michel Angelo's Day and Night, Evening and Morning. The walls were adorned with copies in aquarelle of the most beautiful Italian paintings, and there were portfolios filled with those rolls of silk upon which Japanese painters illustrate the tales of their poets and the episodes of their romances. Less classic in art than in literature, Thiers really preferred the art of Florence and of the Renaissance, but he had acquired a taste for these Japanese artists with their strange mixture of the real and the fantastic. All these marvels of taste have been described by M. Charles Blanc; they can be viewed at the Louvre, Thiers having bequeathed to the State the fruits of his hours of relaxation, as well as those of his toil and his experience.

As might have been foreseen, his retirement did not check the national movement, and the Republican tendency of the elections, for which he had been reproached, became more and more marked. The report of the alliance between the two branches of the House of Bourbon had aroused the public mind. The rural populations were not especially attached to the Republic, but the word " Restoration " exasperated them. The secular hatred of the old serfs of the glebe for the domination of the privileged classes flamed up at the very mention of a dynasty of the Old Régime. The distinction that had hitherto obtained between the House of Orleans and the House of Bourbon now disappeared, and with it the last hope of the Monarchy. The National Assembly did not shut its eyes to the indications furnished by the elections. But it was more disturbed by an event which could have surprised no one who had followed the Count of Chambord through his career as an exiled pretender. Everything indicates that this respectable prince did not wish to reign, but merely to preserve intact his supposed rights, and to bring into subordination the family which, in his eyes, had usurped those rights. Scarcely had he gained this concession, when he wrote a letter the substance of which was that he could not and would not govern the France of the nineteenth century.

Marshal MacMahon, the Ministry, and the Assembly yielded to the inevitable. In politics, he is the best man who first sees the necessity of things, and who undertakes in the nick of time to banish difficulties and augment advantages. Herein lay one of the secrets of Thiers' superiority; his successors found themselves compelled to establish a Republican Constitution under less favorable conditions, inasmuch as they inspired less confidence, as they had embittered party strife, and had furnished their enemies with new grievances and new weapons. This was the most definite result of the 24th of May, 1873, and of the substitution of the Ministry of Messrs. de MacMahon, de Broglie, de La Bouillerie, Tailhand, Depeyre, and Baragnon, for the Ministry of Messrs. Thiers, Jules Simon, de Rémusat, Dufaure, Casimir Périer, and Léon Say.

Thiers took no part in the debate. He contented himself with voting in ironical silence for an excellent Constitution, very similar to the one which he had proposed two years before and which had been the occasion of his fall. He reappeared but once in the Tribune, merely to sustain against General du Barrail, the Minister of War, his opinion touching the construction of the new forts at Paris. This he did with feeling, moderation, and lucidity. It is not unlikely that could Thiers have chosen the occasion for his final speech, this would have been the one he would have preferred. In his last years he had chiefly at heart the things that pertain to the greatness of France in her foreign relations.

After the Constitution had been established, the National Assembly gave way to the two Chambers. The senators were elected in Jan-

uary, 1876, the deputies a little later. Thiers
was elected to both Chambers; for, although
he could not but prefer the second Chamber
as being a better arena for political action, the
people of Belfort had testified their touching
gratitude by choosing him as their senator.
The majority of the Chamber of Deputies
took a decisive course. After a weak pre-
tence of resistance, the President of the Republic was forced to accept as the President
of his Council, whom? M. Jules Simon himself, whose presence in the cabinet of Thiers
had given such umbrage and had seemed to
be one of the principal causes of the 24th of
May. Never has the logic of facts been more
clearly vindicated. It was also doubtless logical that the reactionary coalition should make
another of those efforts whose apparent result
is to check the tide, and whose inevitable result is to hasten it. It appears that, after
some months of administration, M. Jules
Simon involved the social order and religion in new dangers. He was dismissed as
summarily as the Sultan dismisses his Grand
Vizier. After both theory and fact had
shown that the Monarchy was impossible, a
Ministry was formed from the Monarchical
coalition to prorogue and then to dissolve the
Chamber. This is what is known as the *coup*

d'état of the 16th of May, 1877. In sooth, this month of May brings forth strange flowers.

On the day of the dissolution, the Chamber gave Thiers a touching ovation. The Minister of the Interior having been imprudent enough to claim for the Government the honor of delivering the territory, an immense majority of the deputies rose to their feet, stretched out their hands toward Thiers, and an almost unanimous shout proclaimed his right to the name of Liberator. This was the last time that he appeared in public. He was not sick; he bore lightly the weight of his eighty years; but he was enfeebled. The emotion which his physical weakness made him unable to conceal, the tears he shed at hearing himself solemnly hailed by the representatives of the nation as the impersonation of patriotism and of law, enhanced the pathos of the memorable scene.

The dissolution was followed by a period of severe administrative repression designed to influence the elections. Thiers retired to St. Germain, where he was the object of the tender attentions of his wife and of her sister, Mademoiselle Dosne, who made his life easy and happy. There he completed his book of scientific philosophy. Then he turned again to politics, and wrote, for the last time, a summary of the principles which had guided his life, and which had once more been brought into reproach. The publication of this brochure, which every one read, assured victory to the Liberals. But he did not live to see it; he was still holding the pen, when he suddenly and quietly passed away on the 3d of September, 1877. A few days later, the manifesto was published under the editorship of M. Mignet, — a worthy witness of his friend's constancy in opinion and in affection.

All Paris took part in the funeral of the First President of the Republic. During his life the Parisians had cherished a variety of feelings toward him, as was natural in the case of a nervous, changeable people toward a man who changed so little. But as his coffin passed, there was but one sentiment for the dead. Madame Thiers and her friends had declined the public funeral offered by the somewhat embarrassed Ministry. They preferred to trust to that touching and delicate respect for the dead which is a peculiar virtue of the Parisians, to those memories which made this "little bourgeois," as the people called him, the representative of the whole middle class. Not his least claim to our admiration is the fact that this ardent publicist, this impassioned historian, this intelligent orator, invariably upheld those ideas of wise and liberal good sense which, after all, constitute the distinctive mark of the French middle class.

Measure, sobriety, taste pointed with wit, — these are indeed the qualities that the French name represents throughout the civilized world. They are our pride and our glory; to justify our claim to them it is enough that men like Thiers should have borne the name of Frenchman. Our history is too often characterized by excess and violence. Are we not the nation of the Jacquerie and of the Dragonnades? Did we not push religious rancor to the massacre of St. Bartholomew, flattery of monarchs to idolatry under Louis XIV., political fury to the Reign of Terror, love of glory to the Retreat from Moscow, socialist theories to the Insurrection of June, 1848, the spirit of reaction to the selfishness of the Second Empire, anarchy to the Commune? And that respectable National Assembly, — straining toward the goal of Monarchical restoration, unmindful of the past, blind to the present, and careless of what might be the purposes of those whom it would have conducted to the throne, — was its forgetfulness on the 24th of May, of so many services and good counsels, an evidence of sobriety and moderation? Surely Shakspeare were better fitted than any of our classical poets to celebrate such events! Nevertheless, it is by these

poets, and by such of our historians and statesmen as resemble them, that we are best represented in the Congress of Nations. Some
great men, scattered here and there through the
centuries, have saved our honor. Montaigne,
Sully, Henry IV., Molière, Colbert, Vauban,
Montesquieu, Voltaire, Turgot,—these are the
representatives of the French mind and of the
French language. In this select company posterity will assign a place, and a lofty one, to
Louis Adolphe Thiers.

INDEX.[1]

Aix, Academy of, unwilling to award its prize to Thiers, 16.

Alexander II., Tsar, Thiers' mission to, 181, 184-187.

Algeria, a school of war for the French, 68-70.

Ambition, Thiers' relative freedom from, 82, 83.

America, North and South, France must choose between, 107.

Andrieux, François, Thiers' Academic address upon, 73.

Angoulême, Duke of, commands French army of intervention in Spain in 1823, 13.

Armistice (the) between France and Germany, proposed by the Tsar, 186; by other powers, 187; Gambetta and the Delegation consent to, 188, 189; the Paris government consents to, 191, 192; the people of Paris object to, 192, 193; Thiers' negotiations with Bismarck concerning, 193-197.

Arts, fine, Thiers writes upon, 23; his taste for, 224-226.

Augustus, the Emperor, his usurpation like that of Napoleon III., 125, 126; Tacitus' remark applicable to the two Napoleons, 135.

Aumale, Duke of, his service to the Republic, 205.

Austria, mistake of the Empire touching, 157; Thiers' mission to, 183, 184.

Balzac, Honoré de, unfortunate influence of his novels upon social and political ideals, 91-93; similarity of his heroes to the masters of France after the *coup d'état*, 126.

Banquets, campaign of, 95-97.

Barante, Baron, quoted, 94.

Barrot, Odilon, radical leader, 82; Guizot's epigram upon, 84; moderate opposition to Guizot ministry, 89; repugnance to the campaign of banquets, 96.

Bazaine, Marshal, unfortunate results of his surrender, 189.

Belfort, city of, Thiers rescues it from Germany, 201; its gratitude, 229.

Bellamy, Miss, biography by Thiers, 36.

Benedetti, Count Vincent, 165, 166.

Bérard, M., on the force of "fixed situation," 103.

Berger, M., Thiers' faithful shepherd, 19.

Berryer, P. A., a natural declaimer, 60; attitude toward the July Government, 76, 77; description of his oratory, 78; joins the coalition against Minister Molé, 80-82; in the Left with Thiers, 151.

Beust, Count, Thiers' first interview with, 183, 184; second interview, 187.

Bibliography of the writings of Thiers mentioned in this book. *See* Works.

Bismarck, Chancellor of the North German Confederation, excluded by the Ollivier ministry from the Hohenzollern negotiations, 164-166; first interview with Thiers at Versailles, 188-190; consents to negotiate with Thiers concerning the armistice, 193, 194; but wishes to treat for peace, 194, 195; his severe conditions, 196; "a barbarian of genius," 200.

Blanc, Charles, his description of Thiers' art collection, 226.

[1] A complete list of Thiers' writings, so far as they are mentioned or cited in this book, is given under the title "Works." All extended quotations are indexed under the headings "Thiers," "Works," and "Quotations." — Tr.

Bodin, M., at first associated with Thiers in the History of the French Revolution, 39.

Boisserée, Sulpiz, article by Thiers on, 36.

Bonaparte. See Napoleon.

Bonaparte, Prince Louis, plays the part of a pretender in 1848, 110, 111; Thiers breaks with his own party in order to favor the candidacy of, 111-114; elected President of the French Republic, 114; policy, 119; dismisses General Changarnier, 120; Thiers goes into opposition, 120-122 ; coup d'état, 123-126. (See Napoleon III.)

Bordeaux Compact, 210, 219.

Bourbon, House of, opposition to constitutional freedom, 14; its claim of legitimacy the great obstacle to freedom, 33; revolutionary character of their procedure, 56; Thiers upon their boasted legitimacy (quotation), 77, 78; their attitude in 1848 as represented by Falloux, 113, 114; their attitude under the Third Republic, 213; why they sacrificed Martignac and Ollivier, 213, 214; alliance with the House of Orleans, 227.

Broglie, Duke Victor de, opposition to the Bourbon monarchy, 30; characterization of the Doctrinaires, 30, 31; opinion of contemporary literature, 53; famous words about the July Revolution, 53; remark to a signer of Thiers' manifesto, 55; with Thiers in the Soult ministry, 64; republicanism, 100; his part in the Liberal Conference of 1863, 144-146; quoted, 160.

Brunnow, M. de, Russian Ambassador at London, 181.

Buffet, L. J., Finance Minister under Ollivier, 160; the first to resign, 161.

Calmon, M., his edition of Thiers' speeches, 11; his prefaces to these speeches, 64, 153.

Campaign of banquets, Thiers' opposition to, 95-97.

Canouville, M. de, compares Thiers with Napoleon, 69, 70.

Carnot, L. H., attitude toward the Empire, 145.

Carrel, Armand, gets credit for a notable passage by Thiers, 36.

Catholic party. See Clergy.

Cavaignac, General, victory over the insurrection of June, 1848, 110; candidate for the presidency of the Republic, 111; attitude toward the Empire, 145.

Cayla, Madame de, reputed mistress of Louis XVIII., 22.

Chambord, Count of, renounces the hope of the crown, 227.

Changarnier, General, dismissed by President Bonaparte, 120.

Charles X., King of France, characterized, 35; what he did for Thiers, 45.

Charles XII. of Sweden, Voltaire's History of, 45.

Charter, constitutional, of June, 1814, attitude of the Restoration, monarchy toward, 27-29.

Chénier, André, Thiers distantly related to, 16.

Church, Roman Catholic. See Clergy.

Clergy, the Roman Catholic, their hostility to freedom under the Restoration, 27; victory in the contest with the University concerning secondary instruction, 90, 91; Thiers' concessions to them in 1849 and 1850, 115-119.

Coalition of Guizot, Thiers, Berryer, and Barrot against Minister Molé, 80-82.

Colbert, a representative Frenchman, 233.

Cologne Cathedral, article by Thiers on, 36.

Common-sense, Thiers on, 109.

Commune (the), how Thiers met it, 206, 210; destruction of his house and collections by, 224, 225.

Compact of Bordeaux, 210, 219.

Conservatives, French Tories, Guizot their leader, 83; far less disposed than he to concede reforms, 89-91; forlorn hope of this party, 92, 93; exclusiveness and intolerance of, 213, 214.

Constitution, proposed revision in 1851, 122; the Emperor's modification of that of 1852, 142-144; that of 1869 voted by plebiscite, 161; Thiers' postponement of the discussion of that of the Third Republic, 202, 204, 205, 219; its first article, 216.

"Constitutionnel," the, contains an extract from Thiers' prize essay, 17; first journal for which Thiers wrote, 21; character of his articles, 22, 23; the organ of Thiers' political ideas, 32.

Consulate and Empire, History of. See History.

Conversation, brilliancy of Thiers', 67-69; in the time of the Third Empire, 129-131; Thiers' use of in preparing his speeches, 153.

"Corinne." Madame de Staël's romance, Thiers' criticism of, 23-25.

Coup d'État (of Dec. 1851), 123-126; its influence on Thiers' judgment of the 18th Brumaire, 135.

Coup d'État (of May, 1877), 229, 230.

Cousin, Victor, taunts Thiers with ignorance of Greek, 118.

Crimean War (the), Thiers' attitude concerning, 132.

"Defence of Property," book by Thiers, 108.

Delacroix, his genius divined by Thiers, 23.

Delegation of Tours, 187, 188, 189, 190.

Disraeli, Benjamin, plagiarism from Thiers, 36.

Doctrinaires, their attitude toward the Bourbon monarchy, 30, 31; Thiers' divergence from them, 31-33.

Dosne, Mlle., Thiers' sister-in-law, 230.

Doudan, X., description of Thiers' conversation quoted and criticised, 68-71; phrase quoted, 164.

Duchies, question of the, Thiers' advice concerning, 157.

Dufaure, Jules, political principles, 102; refuses to follow Thiers' leadership in 1848, 111; accepts a portfolio under Thiers, 201.

Dupin (the Elder), on the confiscation of the Orleans estates, 125.

Duval, Jules, editor "Journal des Débats," 182.

Duvergier de Hauranne, Prosper, discusses Algiers with Thiers, 69; republicanism, 100; exiled with Thiers in December, 1851, 124.

Education Bill of 1850, alliance of Thiers and Falloux in favor of, 117-119.

Empire, Consulate and, History of. See History.

Empire, the Second (1851-1870). See Napoleon III.

Empress (the). See Eugénie.

England, her constitution regarded by Thiers as a model for France, 32, 34; Thiers' mission to, 180, 181.

Eugénie, Empress of France, her marriage, 127; seeks the aid of Thiers, 173-175.

Falloux, Alfred de, blame of Thiers in his memoirs, 113; alliance with Thiers against the University, 117-119.

Favre, Jules, 76 (foot-note); one of the Five, 144; his speaking characterized, 151; proposes to Thiers the mission to the neutral powers, 179; rendezvous with Thiers, 196.

February Revolution (year 1848), lack of moral justification, 99; endangered civilization, 103.

Female sex. See Women.

Ferdinand VII., King of Spain, reinstated by France in 1823, 14.

Ferry, Jules, deputy in 1869, 160; with Picard rescues the Trochu ministry, 195.

Finance, Thiers' papers and speeches on, 58, 59.

Florence and Venice contrasted by Thiers, 158, 159.

Fourrichon, Admiral, Minister of War after the 4th of September, 182.

Freedom, political, relation to moral freedom, 58; Thiers' definition of, 154.

French Academy, Thiers' reception into, 73-75.

French representative men, 233.

French traits, 232.

Gambetta, Léon, elected deputy in 1869, 160; head of the war party at Tours, 188; his improvised armies, 197; sacrificed the interests of the Republic, 198.

Gautier, Théophile, his love of art for art's sake, 52.

Gérard, the painter, Thiers comments upon his picture of Corinne inspired, 23.

Gladstone, W. E., unwillingness to make promises to Thiers, 181.

"Globe," the, Thiers does the art criticism for, 23; organ of the Doctrinaire opposition to the Bourbon monarchy, 30, 31.

Gortschakoff, Prince, Thiers' interviews with, 185, 186.

Government of Louis Philippe. See July Government.

Gramont, Duke of, Foreign Minister under Ollivier, 163; his "hussar-diplomacy," 164-167; his mistake about Austria, 184.

Granville, Lord, reception of Thiers, 180.

Greek, study of, Thiers complains of the time given to, 118.

Guicciardini, cited by Thiers, 155.

Guizot, F. P. G., his oratory, 60; his oratory compared with that of Thiers, 63; elected to the Academy the year after Thiers, 75; leader of the coalition against the Molé ministry, 81, 82; becomes leader of the timid conservatives, 83, 84; ambassador to England under Thiers, 85; succeeds Thiers as prime minister, 86; resists electoral reform, 87; remark concerning Thiers, 88; more liberal than his party, 89; quoted, 90; note to Metternich (quoted), 94, 95; quoted, 116; attacks the Education Bill of 1850, 119; his party spirit, 213.

HAUBERSART, M. de, discusses Algiers with Thiers, 69.

Hauranne. *See* Duvergier.

Henry IV., Thiers' policy identical with that of, 212; a representative Frenchman, 233.

" History of the Consulate and the Empire," the most splendid monument of contemporary literature, 10; account and criticism of, 135–140; Metternich's estimate, 141.

" History of the French Revolution," account and criticism of, 38–45.

Hohenzollern, Leopold, Prince of, crown of Spain offered to, 164.

House in the Place St. George, Thiers' art collection in, 224–226.

Hugo, Victor, his tardy justice to Louis Philippe, 50; quoted, 194, 195.

INSTRUCTION, secondary, 90. (*See* Education Bill.)

Italy, Thiers' attitude toward, 157; graceful remarks concerning, (quoted), 158, 159; eventful day on which he first set foot on her soil, 183; his interview with her king, 187.

JAPANESE art, Thiers' fancy for, 226.

" Jérôme Paturot " (novel by Reybaud), description of Thiers' oratory quoted from, 71, 72.

July Government, its ill-fortune, 47–49; attitude of imaginative writers toward, 49–53; Thiers' brochure on, 55–58; golden era of, 78, 79; hostility of the clerical party to, 91; injury inflicted by Balzac's novels upon, 92–94; overthrown, 98; a habitable republic, 99; regretted by Thiers, 102; hostility of the Catholic clergy to, 116, 117; Thiers' later feeling toward, 149; why sacrificed by the conservatives, 213.

July Revolution (year 1830), why acceptable to the people, 34; occasion and nature, 46; a noble spectacle, 53; share of Thiers in, 54–57.

LAFAYETTE, his policy of conspiracy against the Bourbon monarchy, 28, 29.

Laffitte, Jacques, his use of Thiers' financial papers, 58.

Lagarde, Denis, the Emperor's ironical remark concerning, 143.

Lamartine, Alphonse de, his History of the Girondins, 40, 42; his oratory, 60; opposed to war in 1848, 104.

Law, John, study of by Thiers, 36.

Lecomte, General, the Commune begins with his murder, 206.

Left Centre. *See* Liberal party.

Legitimate monarchy and legitimacy. *See* Bourbon.

Lemoinne, John, his anecdote of Thiers, 53.

Leopold, Prince of Hohenzollern, crown of Spain offered to, 164.

Liberal party, how it suffered by the French Revolution, 41, 42; becomes a Whig party with Thiers as leader, 83; moderation of the liberal opposition to the Guizot ministry, 86–89; the caucus of 1863, 144–146; Thiers states its mission under the Empire, 149; Jules Simon describes its attitude under the Third Republic, 202–204; Thiers reconciles it to the Republic, 204–206.

Liberal Union (the), 130, 131, 204.

Liberty. *See* Freedom.

Literature, imaginative, hostile to the July Government, 49–53; social influence exemplified in the case of Balzac, 91–93.

Littré, E., credits a notable passage by Thiers to Armand Carrel, 36.

Louis XVIII., Thiers offends the literary vanity of, 21.

Louis Philippe (at first the Duke of Orleans), his qualification for the throne, 33, 34; happily named, 46; anecdote of, 47, 48; Victor Hugo's tardy justice to, 50; brought back to Paris by Thiers, 54; summons

Thiers and takes flight, 93; regarded as a persecutor of the clergy, 116.

MACHIAVELLI, cited by Thiers, 154.
MacMahon, Marshal, Thiers opposes his movement that ended in Sedan, 175; should have fallen back upon Paris, 191; his ministry after Thiers' resignation, 228; his *coup d'état*, 229, 230.
Mérimée, Prosper, his relation to Napoleon III., 51; attempts to mediate between the Emperor and Thiers, 132, 133; negotiates with Thiers on behalf of the Empress, 173, 174.
Metternich, Prince of, obliged to flee in 1848, 104; irritation with the Pope in 1849, 115; estimate of Thiers' Consulate and Empire (quoted), 141.
Mexican expedition (the), 155, 156.
Mignet, François, Thiers' lifelong intimacy with, 18-20; prosecuted for freedom of speech, 35; a partisan of the Revolution, 43; editor of Thiers' last political work, 231.
Milo of Crotona, how he pressed the pomegranate, 103.
Mirabeau, Marquis, Thiers' alleged imitation of, 59, 60.
Molé, M., the coalition of party chiefs against his ministry, 79-82.
Molière, J. B. P., quoted to describe Thiers, 66, 67; quoted, 201; a representative Frenchman, 233.
"Monarchy of 1830, The," brochure by Thiers, 55-58.
Monarchy of July, or of Louis Philippe. *See* July Government.
Montaigne, a representative Frenchman, 233.
Montalembert, Count of, failure of Guizot to conciliate him, 91.
Montesquieu, on usurpation in a free state, 125, 126; a representative Frenchman, 233.
Morality, relation to politics, 57, 58.
Musset, Alfred de, quoted, 138.

NAPOLEON BONAPARTE, compared and contrasted with Thiers, 70, 71; Thiers' eulogy of (quotation), 74, 75; Thiers' consistent judgment of his character, 135, 136; Thiers' excessive admiration for, 136-138; not open to suggestions, 215.
Napoleon III., the *coup d'état*, 123-126; his reign a series of surprises, 126, 127; and of novel proposals, 128; mistook day-dreaming for meditation, 128, 129; *good* society has no need of a savior, 129-131; his way of receiving Thiers' suggestions, 132, 133; did he cause Thiers to think worse of his uncle? 135, 136; his modifications in the Constitution of 1852, 142-144; his "unrecognized incapacity," 156; his foreign policy, 156-158; deceives himself by universal suffrage, 159; his reform ministry, 160-163; picks a quarrel with Germany, 163-166; fears Thiers was right, 173; the Empress invokes the aid of Thiers, 173-175; "vacancy of the throne," 175; hostility of the Austrians to, 184. (*See* Bonaparte, Prince Louis.)
Nodier, Charles, competitor with Thiers for election to the Academy, 73.

OLLIVIER, Émile, one of the Five, 144; his eloquence characterized, 151; head of the reform ministry, 160; his blindness, 161, 162; joins the Bonapartists, 166; his weakness described by Thiers, 171.
Orleans, Duke of. *See* Louis Philippe.
Orleans, House of. *See* Louis Philippe; July Government.
Orleans Monarchy. *See* July Government.
Orleans, Princes of, their services in organizing the French army, 86; their estates confiscated by Napoleon III., 125; Thiers' reference to the fact, 149; their behavior under the Third Republic, 205, 206; their concession to the Count of Chambord, 227.

PALMERSTON, Lord, on the Schleswig-Holstein question, 157.
Paris, condition of after the fall of Metz, 191; people of, oppose the armistice, 192, 193; day of the 31st October at, 193; surrender of, 197, 198; its feeling for Thiers, 231.
Parliamentary reform, demanded by Thiers and refused by Guizot, 88, 89.
Pasteur, Louis, Thiers follows his researches, 133.
"Paturot, Jérôme" (novel by Reybaud). Description of Thiers' oratory, 71, 72.

Pericles, Thucydides' words concerning (quoted), 200.
Périer, Casimir, his ministry, 61; Thiers decides to support him, 62.
Pessard, Hector, description of Thiers as president, 211.
Picard, Ernest, one of the Five, 144; characterized, 151; quoted, 159; with Ferry rescues the Trochu ministry, 195.
Plateau, M., Thiers repeats his fine experiment, 133.
Politics, related to morality, 57, 58.
Polybius, cited by Thiers, 155.
Prévost-Paradol, Minister to the United States, 160.
" Property, Defence of," book by Thiers, 108.
Proudhon, Pierre Joseph, Thiers' report and speeches on his propositions and theories, 109, 110.
Prussia, Thiers points out her sudden accession of strength (quotation), 163; her self-respect wounded by the Ollivier ministry, 164, 165; declaration of war with, 166; Thiers' opinion as to the true course of the ministry toward (quoted), 170.
Pyat, Félix, tries to overthrow the Government of Defence, 195.
" Pyrenees (the) and the South of France during the Months of November and December, 1822," Thiers' first book, 13-16, 21.

QUESTORS, proposition of in 1851, 122, 123.
Quotations from Thiers' writings, 23, 36, 37, 73, 77, 101, 105, 109, 121, 148, 154, 155, 158, 163, 168, 170, 176, 208, 217. (See Works.)

RADICALISM, Thiers' hostility to (quotation), 101.
Rémusat, Count of (father of the author), Thiers' intimacy with, 97; refuses to follow Thiers' leadership in 1848, 111; exiled with Thiers in December, 1851, 124; Minister of Foreign Affairs under Thiers, 220.
Republic of 1848, people poorly prepared for, 99; attitude of Thiers toward, 100-103; how it escaped the dangers of war, 104, 105.
Republic, the Third, proclaimed by the masses, 177, 178; Thiers at its head, 198; in its name he reconstructs the government and negotiates peace, 201-210; difference between the Republic and Republican government, 220.
Republican party, reconciled by Thiers to the old Liberal party, 204, 205; why he would not cut off its tail, 214.
Restoration of the House of Bourbon in France, 14; hostility to the principles of the Revolution, 26-29; why Martignac was abandoned under, 213; the fear of it under the Third Republic, 226, 227.
Revolution, the French, its useful results, 26, 37, 38 (quotation); Thiers' History of, 38-45; reason for its failure, 57; Thiers an adherent of (quotation), 101.
Revolution of February, 1848. See February Revolution.
Revolution of July, 1830. See July Revolution.
Reybaud, Louis, quotation from his novel of " Jérôme Paturot," 71, 72.
Rhetoric, inefficacy of its precepts, 9, 152; Thiers' contribution to, 152, 153.
" Rolla," by Alfred de Musset, quoted, 138.
Roman Catholic party. See Clergy.
Roman expedition, Thiers defends the credits for, 115.
Romanticism, Thiers' opinion of, 53.
Rouher, Eugène, on the Mexican expedition, 156; expounds the foreign policy of the Empire, 156.
Russia, Thiers' mission to, 181, 184-187.

SACY, S. U. S. de, his classical tastes commended by Thiers, 53.
Saint-Cyr, Marshal Gouvion, article by Thiers on, 36.
Sainte-Beuve, debt of modern criticism to, 37; on Thiers' description of the Mountain, 42; quoted, 79; estimate of Thiers' Consulate and Empire, 135.
Saint-Hilaire, Barthélemy, opposes the Education Bill of 1850, 119; elected deputy in 1869, 160.
Sardou, Victorien, his hero the Engineer, 50.
Say, Léon, on Thiers as a financier, 211.
Schleswig - Holstein, Thiers' advice concerning, 157.
Scientific studies, Thiers blames the prominence allowed them by the University, 118; his later interest in, 133, 134.

Secondary instruction, bill of 1844 concerning, 90. (*See* Education Bill.)

Sense, common, Thiers on, 109.

Sex, the. *See* Women.

Shakspeare, his fitness to celebrate French violence, 232.

Simiane, Madame de, her comparison between the royalists and the party of Lafayette, 29.

Simon, Jules, opposes the Education Bill of 1850, 119; his oratory described, 151; his description of the party of Thiers, 203, 204; obnoxious declaration about Thiers, 221; prime minister in 1876, 229; dismissal by MacMahon, 229, 230.

Socialism, Thiers' refutation of Proudhon's, 109.

Soldier (the), Thiers' estimate of the ability required for the profession of (quotation), 36, 37; his opinion of Algiers as a school for, 68–70; the life of (quotation), 217, 218.

Soult, Marshal, Thiers in his ministry, 64.

Spain, Invasion of by France in 1823, 13–15.

Speeches of Thiers, Calmon's edition, 11, 64, 153; method of preparation, 152, 153. (*See* Quotations; Works.)

Staël, Madame de, Thiers' criticism of, 23–25.

Style, characteristics of Thiers', 9–11, 139, 140.

Suffrage, its extension demanded by Thiers and refused by Guizot, 87; rise of universal, 98.

Sully, a representative Frenchman, 233.

"TABLETTES UNIVERSELLES," weekly review to which Thiers contributed, 21; bought up by the Bourbon ministry, 22.

Tacitus, Guizot's unfortunate quotation from, 82; quoted, 135.

Talleyrand, befriends Thiers, 21; on the *salons* of the Revolution, 129.

Terror, Reign of, influence in French politics, 41, 42.

Thiers, Louis Adolphe (1797–1877), place in French literature, 9–12; book on the Pyrenees and the south of France, 13; birth and education, 16; early friendship with Mignet, 18–20; writes for the "Constitutionnel," 21–23; estimate of Madame de Staël (quoted), 23–25;

political principles and practice under the Restoration Monarchy, 31–34; success of his policy, 35; on the art of war (quoted), 36, 37; on the French Revolution (quoted), 37, 38; "History of the French Revolution," 38–45; share in the Revolution of July, 1830, 54–57; deputy and Under-Secretary of State, 58; unpromising *début* in the Chamber, 59; first success as a speaker, 61–64; Minister of the Interior under Marshal Soult, 64; merits and defects of his speeches, 64, 65; boldness in action, 66; brilliancy in conversation, 67–69; simple and conversational style of his oratory, 71–73; installation speech at the French Academy (quoted), 73–75; on the legitimate monarchy (quoted), 77; joins the coalition against the Molé ministry, 81; ambition, 82, 83; opposition to Guizot, 83–91; blindness to the signs of the times in 1847, 93–95; inaction at the crisis of February, 1848, 96–98; attitude toward the Republic, 100; quoted, 101; loyalty to the fallen Monarchy, 102, 103; discouragement shown by letter to a friend, 105, 106; again a deputy, 106; on the Finance Committee, 107; "Defence of Property," 108; on common-sense (quoted), 109; refutes Proudhon's socialism, 109; favors the candidacy of Bonaparte, 112; defends the Roman expedition, 115; alliance with the clergy against the University, 116–119; resumes the leadership of the Liberal party, 120; quotation from his speech, 121; supports the Republic against the encroachments of Bonaparte, 122; exile, 124–126; attitude toward the Empire, 129–131; social life, 131; patriotism, 132; scientific studies, 133, 134; "History of the Consulate and the Empire," 135; estimate of Napoleon, 135–138; defects and excellencies of his historical method, 138–141; enters the Corps Législatif in 1863, 144; first great speech, 147; the same analyzed and quoted, 148–150; prudent and moderate opposition to the Empire, 150–152; method of preparing a speech, 152, 153; definition of a free country (quoted), 154; vigilance the price of national safety (quoted), 155; sharp opposition to imperial foreign policy, 155-158; graceful passage on Italy (quoted), 158, 159; supports the reform ministry of Ollivier, 160; demands that the army be strengthened, 162; points out the strength of Prussia (quotation), 163; firmly opposes the declaration of war, 166-168; speech of July 15, 1870 (quoted), 168, 169; letter to a friend describing the scene in the Chamber, 170-172; overtures of the Empress, 173, 174; member of the Council of Defence, 174; Sedan, 175; describes the overthrow of the Empire by the Chamber (quotation), 176; Embassy to all the great powers, 179; at London, 180, 181; at Vienna, 183, 184; at St. Petersburg, 184-186; at Florence, 187; returns to Tours, 187, 188; negotiations with Bismarck looking to an armistice, 188-197; head of the French Republic, 198; first citizen, 200; moderate liberal attitude during the critical and formative period of the Republic, 202-206; transfers the seat of government to Versailles, 206, 207; promises not to destroy the Republic (quotation), 208; pledges himself to the Republic, 209; great achievements, 210; greatness as an administrator, 211, 212; management of the Assembly, 212-216; description of his appearance in the Chamber, 216, 217; quotation on the soldier's life from a speech on recruitment, 217, 218; completes the liberation of French soil, 218-220; resignation, 221, 222; in retirement, 223; works of art adorning his house, 224-226; receives an ovation from the Chamber, 230; final literary work, 230, 231; death and funeral, 231; one of the first representatives of the French mind, 232, 233. (*See* Quotations; Works.)

Thiers, Madame, 230, 231.

Thomas, General Clément, his murder, 206.

Thucydides, words about Pericles applied to Thiers, 200.

Thureau-Dangin, M., history of the July Government by, 49.

Tocqueville, Alexis de, political principles, 102; defection from Thiers, 111.

Tours, Delegation of. *See* Delegation.

Turgot, a representative Frenchman, 233.

ULTRAMONTANE party. *See* Clergy.

Union, the Liberal, 130, 131.

Universal suffrage. *See* Suffrage.

University of France (the), the Guizot ministry sacrifice it to the clergy, 90, 91; alliance of Thiers and Falloux against, 117-119.

VAUBAN, a representative Frenchman, 233.

Vauvenargues, Thiers' prize discourse upon, 16-18.

Venice, contrasted by Thiers with Florence, 158, 159.

Vernet, Horace, his popularity predicted by Thiers, 23.

Versailles, transference of the seat of Government to, 206, 207.

Victor Emmanuel, King of Italy, Thiers' interview with, 187.

Voltaire, Thiers belongs to his intellectual family, 26; Thiers' style compared with his, 44; Thiers' subject compared with his, 45; Thiers like him in other respects, 65; characteristics which he shared in common with Napoleon and with Thiers, 70; his scientific knowledge and that of Thiers, 134, 135; a representative Frenchman, 233.

WAR, art of. *See* Soldier.

Wellington, Duke of, Thiers' anecdote of, 128

William I., King of Prussia, approves the renunciation of the Spanish crown by Prince Leopold, 164, 165; pressed by the Ollivier ministry, 165, 166.

Women, Thiers' want of esteem for their genius, 25; his gallantry toward, 131; his wife and her sister, 230.

Works of Thiers, general remarks on, 9-12; "The Pyrenees and the South of France during the Months of November and December, 1822," 13-16, 21; prize discourse on Vauvenargues, 16-18; political articles for the "Constitutionnel," 21-23; political bulletins for the "Tablettes Universelles," 21; art criticism for the "Globe" (quotation), 23-25; biography of Miss Bellamy, 36; article on Sulpiz Boisserée, 36;

article on Cologne Cathedral, 36; study of John Law, 36; article on Marshal Saint-Cyr (quoted), 36, 37; article in response to Montlosier (quoted), 37, 38; " History of the French Revolution," 38-45; Protest against the July Ordinances, 54, 55; " The Monarchy of 1830," 55-57; first two speeches on finance, 59, 60; first successful speech, 61; speech on foreign affairs (August, 1831), 62, 63; first ministerial speech, 64; speech upon being received into the Academy (quoted), 73-75; speeches of Dec. 31, 1834, and of Jan. 22, 1835 (quoted), 77, 78; report upon the Education Bill of 1844, 90, 117; speech of Feb. 2, 1848 (quoted), 101; letter of March 3, 1848 (quoted), 105, 106; " Defence of Property," 108; speech of May 6, 1834 (quoted), 109; report and speeches upon Proudhon's theories and proposals, 109, 110; speech in defence of the Italian policy (1849), 115; speech on the first act of the conspiracy of Louis Bonaparte (quoted), 120, 121; speech on the proposition of the Questors (Nov. 1851), 122; unpublished work on scientific philosophy, 134, 230;

" History of the Consulate and the Empire," 135-141; first important speech in the Corps Législatif (quoted), 147-150; definition of a free country (quoted), 154; on political prudence (from the speech of April 13, 1865), 155; on Italy (from the same), 158, 159; speech of March 14, 1867, 157, 158; speech of Jan. 27, 1870, 160, 162; speech of June 30, 1870 (quoted), 162, 163; speech of July 15, 1870 (quoted), 167-169; letter of July 21, 1870 (quoted), 170-172; deposition before the Committee of Inquiry, Sept. 17, 1871 (quoted), 176; account of his mission to the neutral powers, 197; speech to the Assembly at Bordeaux, 206; speech of March 27, 1871, (quoted), 208; speech of April 16, 1835 (quoted), 215; speech on recruitment (June 8, 1872, quoted), 217, 218; message to the Assembly (1872), 218, 219; farewell discourse, 221, 222; his last speech in the Assembly, 228; his summary of his political principles, 230, 231. (*See* Quotations.)

Writers, imaginative, attitude toward the July Government, 49-53.

Writings of Thiers. *See* Works.

THE END.

www.ingramcontent.com/pod-product-compliance
Lightning Source LLC
Chambersburg PA
CBHW030819020726

47499CB00006B/1988